Alizon

Gates

Tor Moor

Torwarsh Villiage

WITHDRAWN
Fairhope Public Library

Estcarp

Gorm

Sulcar
Keep

Sippar

Yle

Place of Wisdom
★

South Keep ✶

Etsford

Es

Lormt

Eyrie of Falconers

Cave of Volt

Verlaine

Randtan

D1253007

Copyright © 1977 by Barbi Johnson

FAIRHOPE PUBLIC LIBRARY

006388

55580

SCIENCE FICTION

Fic
NorT

Norton, Andre
Three against the witch
world.

7.95

DATE DUE

JAN 0 5 1996			
OCT 0 7 1996			
APR 0 7 1997			
MAY 24 1997			
AUG 1 0 1999			
JAN 1 9 2001			
MAY 3 0 2001			
JUL 1 2 2001			

WITHDRAWN
Fairhope Public Library

FAIRHOPE PUBLIC LIBRARY
10 N. Summit St.
Fairhope. Al

The Witch World Novels
of
Andre Norton

*Three Against
the
Witch World*

The Witch World Novels
of
Andre Norton

Witch World
Web of the Witch World
Three Against the Witch World
Warlock of the Witch World
Sorceress of the Witch World
Year of the Unicorn
Spell of the Witch World

SCIENCE FICTION

Fic
Nort

Three Against the
the
Witch World

ANDRE NORTON

55580

Gregg Press

BOSTON

1977

FAIRHOPE PUBLIC LIBRARY
10 N. Summit St.
Fairhope, AL 36532

Three Against the Witch World
Copyright © 1965 by Ace Books, Inc.
All Rights Reserved

This edition published in 1977 by Gregg Press
A Division of G. K. Hall & Co.
by arrangement with Ace Books, Inc.
and with the cooperation of Andre Norton

Jacket and text art by Jack Gaughan
Frontmatter art by Alice Phalen
Endleave maps by Barbi Johnson

Library of Congress Cataloging in Publication Data

Norton, Andre.
Three against the Witch World.

(The Witch World novels of Andre Norton)
Reprint of the ed. published by Ace Books, New York.
I. Title. II. Series: Norton, Andre. The Witch
World novels of Andre Norton.
PZ3.N8187Th5 [PS3527.0625] 813'.5'2 77-23202
ISBN 0-8398-2358-4

Manufactured in the United States of America

*Three Against
the
Witch World*

I

I AM NO song-smith to forge a blade of chant to send men roaring into battle, as the bards of the Sulcar ships do when those sea-serpents nose into enemy ports. Nor can I use words with care as men carve out stones for the building of a strong, years-standing, keep wall, that those generations following may wonder at their industry and skill. Yet when a man passes through great times, or faces action such as few dream on, there awakes within him the desire to set down, even limpingly, his part in those acts so that those who come after him to warm his high seat, lift his sword, light the fire on his hearth, may better understand what he and his fellows wrought that they might do these same things after the passing of time.

Thus do I write out the truth of the Three against Estcarp, and what chanced when they ventured to break a spell which had lain more than a thousand years on the

THREE AGAINST THE WITCH WORLD

Old Race, to darken minds and blot out the past. Three of us in the beginning, only three, Kyllan, Kemoc, and Kaththea. We were not fully of the Old Race, and in that lay both our sorrow and our salvation. From the hours of our birth we were set apart, for we were the House of Tregarth.

Our mother was the Lady Jaelithe who had been a Woman of Power, one of the Witches, able to summon, send and use forces beyond common reckoning. But it was also true that, contrary to all former knowledge, though she lay with our father, the Lord Warder Simon, and brought forth us three in a single birth, yet she lost not that gift which cannot be measured by sight nor touch.

And, though the Council never returned to her her Jewel, forfeited at the hour of her marriage, yet they were also forced to admit that she was still a Witch, though not one of their fellowship.

And he who was our father was also not to be measured by any of the age-old laws and customs. For he was out of another age and time, entering into Estcarp by one of the Gates. In his own world he had been a warrior, one giving orders to be obeyed by other men. But he fell into a trap of ill fortune, and those who were his enemies sniffed at his heels in such numbers that he could not stand and meet them blade to blade. Thus he was hunted until he found the Gate and came into Estcarp, and so also into the war against the Kolder.

But by him and my mother there came also the end of Kolder. And the House of Tregarth thereafter had no little honor. For Simon and the Lady Jaelithe went up against the Kolder in their own secret place, and closed *their* Gate through which that scourge had come upon us. And of this there has already been sung many songs.

But though the Kolder evil was gone, the stain lingered and Estcarp continued to gasp for life as her enemies, ringing her about, nibbled eternally at her tattered borders. This was a twilight world, for which would come no morning, and we were born into the dusk of life.

Our triple birth was without precedent among the Old

Race. When our mother was brought to bed on the last day of the dying year, she sang warrior spells, determined that that one who would enter into life would be a fighter such as was needed in this dark hour. Thus came I, crying as if already all the sorrows of a dim and forbidding future shadowed me.

Yet my mother's labor was not at an end. And there was such concern for her that I was hurriedly tended and put to one side. Her travail continued through the hours, until it would seem that she and that other life, still within her, would depart through the last gate of all.

Then there came a stranger to the Ward Keep, a woman walking on her own two dusty feet. In the courtyard she lifted up her voice, saying she was one sent and that her mission lay with the Lady Jaelithe. By that time so great was my father's fear that he ordered her brought in.

From under her cloak she drew a sword, the blade of it bright in the light, a glittering, icy thing, cold with the burden of killing metal. Holding this before my mother's eyes, she began to chant, and from that moment it was as if all the anxious ones gathered in that chamber were bound with ties they could not break. But the Lady Jaelithe rose out of the sea of pain and haunted dreams which held her, and she too gave voice. Wild raving they thought those words of hers as she said:

"Warrior, sage, witch—three—one—I will this! Each a gift, Together—one and great—apart far less!"

And in the second hour of the new year there came forth my brother, and then my sister, close together as if they were linked by a tie. But so great was my mother's exhaustion that her life was feared for. The woman who had made the birth magic put aside the sword quickly and took up the children as if that was her full right—and, because of my mother's collapse, none disputed her.

Thus Anghart of the Falconer village became our nurse and foster mother and had the first shaping of us in this world. She was an exile from her people, since she had revolted against their harsh code and departed by night from their woman village. For the Falconers, those strange fighting men, had their own customs, unnatural in the eyes of the Old Race whose women hold great power and authority. So repugnant were these customs to the Witches of Estcarp that they had refused the Falconers settlement land when they had come, centuries earlier, from over seas. Thus now the Hold of the Falconers was in the high mountains, a no-man's land border country between Estcarp and Karsten.

Among this people the males dwelt apart, living only for war and raiding, having more affection and kinship with their scout hawks then they did with their women. The latter were quartered in valley villages, to which certain selected men went at seasons to establish that their race did not die out. But upon the birth of children there was a ruthless judging, and Anghart's newly born son had been slain, since he had a crippled foot. So she came to the South Keep, but why she chose that day and hour, and seemed to have foreknowledge of our mother's need, she never said. Nor did any choose to ask her, for to most in the Keep she turned a grim, closed face.

But to us she was warmth, and love, and the mother the Lady Jaelithe could not be. Since from the hour of the last birth my mother sank into a trance of sorts and thus she lay day after day, eating when food was put in her mouth, aware of nothing about her. And this passed for several months. My father appealed to the Witches, but in return he received only a cold message—that Jaelithe had seen fit to follow her own path always, and. that they did not meddle in the matters of fate, nor could they reach one who had gone long and far down an alien way.

Upon this saying my father grew silent and grim in his turn. He led his Borderers out on wild forays, showing a love of steel play and bloodletting new to him. And they said of him that he was willfully seeking yet another road and that led to the Black Gate. Of us he took no note, save to ask from time to time how we fared—absently, as if our welfare was that of strangers, no real concern to him.

THREE AGAINST THE WITCH WORLD

It was heading into another year when the Lady Jaelithe at last roused. Then she was still weak and slipped easily into sleep when overtired. Also she seemed shadowed, as if some unhappiness she could not name haunted her mind. At length this wore away and there was a lightsome time, if brief, when the Seneschel Koris and his wife, the Lady Loyse, came to South Keep at the waning of the year to make merry, since the almost ceaseless war had been brought to an uneasy truce and for the first time in years there was no flame nor fast riding along either border, neither north to face the wolves of Alizon nor south where the anarchy in Karsten was a constant boil and bubble of raid and counter-raid.

But that was only a short breathing space. For it was four months into the new year when the threat of Pagar came into being. Karsten had been a wide battle field for many lords and would-be rulers since Duke Yvian had been killed during the Kolder war. To that wracked duchy the Lady Loyse had a claim. Wedded by force—axe marriage —to the Duke, she had never ruled. But on his death she might have raised his standard. However, there was no tie between her and a country in which she had suffered much. Loving Koris, she had thankfully tossed away any rights over Karsten. And the policy of Estcarp, to hold and maintain the old kingdom, not to carry war to its neighbors, suited her well. Also Koris and Simon, both bolstering as well as they could the dwindling might of the Old Race, saw no advantage in embroilment abroad, but much gain in the anarchy which would keep one of their enemies employed elsewhere.

Now what they had foreseen came to pass. Starting as a small holder in the far south, Pagar of Geen began to gather followers and establish himself, first as a lord of two southern provinces, then acclaimed by the men of the city of Kars of their own free will, the ruined merchants there willing to declare for any one likely to reestablish peace. By the end of our birth year Pagar was strong enough to risk battle against a confederation of rivals. And four

9

months later he was proclaimed Duke, even along the border.

He came to rule in a country devastated by the worst sort of war, a civil struggle. His followers were a motley and hard-to-control crew. Many were mercenaries, and the loot which had drawn them under his banner must now be replaced by wages or they would go elsewhere to plunder.

Thus Pagar did as my father and Koris had expected: he looked outside his borders for a cause to unite his followers and provide the means for rebuilding his duchy. And where he looked was north. Estcarp had always been feared. Yvian, under the suggestion of the Kolder, had outlawed and massacred those of the Old Race who had founded Karsten in days so far distant that no man could name the date. They had died—hard—or they had fled, across the mountains to their kin. And behind they left a burden of guilt and fear. None in Karsten ever really believed that Estcarp would not some day move to avenge those deaths. Now Pagar need only play slightly on that emotion and he had a crusade to occupy his fighters and unite the duchy firmly behind him.

Still, Estcarp was a formidable foe and one Pagar desired to test somewhat before he committed himself. Not only were the Old Race dour and respected fighting men, but the Witches of Estcarp used the Power in ways no outsider could understand, and which were the more dreaded for that very reason. In addition there was a firm and unbreakable alliance between Estcarp and the Sulcarmen —those dreaded sea rovers who already had raided Alizon into a truce and a sullen licking of sore wounds. They were as ready to turn their serpent ships southward and bite along Karsten's open coast line, and that would arouse the merchants of Kars to rebellion.

So Pagar had to ·prepare his holy war quietly. Border raiding began that summer, but never in such strength that the Falconers and the Borderers my father commanded could not easily control. Yet many small raids, even though easily beaten back, can gnaw at the warding forces. A few men lost here, one or two there—the sum mounts and is a steady drain. As my father early knew.

Estcarp's answer was loosing of the Sulcar fleets. And that did give Pagar to think. Hostovrul gathered twenty ships, rode out a storm by spectacular seamanship, and broke the river patrol, to raid into Kars itself, with such success that he left the new Duke unsteady for another full year. And then there was an insurrection in the south from whence Pagar had come, led by his own half-brother, to keep the Duke further engaged. Thus three years, maybe more, were won from the threat of chaos, and the twilight of Estcarp did not slide into night as quickly as the Old Race had feared.

During these years of maneuvering the three of us were taken from the fortress of our birth—but not to Es, for both our father and mother held aloof from the city where the Council reigned. The lady Loyse established a home in a small manor-garth of Etsford, and welcomed us into her household. Anghart was still the center of our lives, and she made an acceptable alliance with the mistress of Etsford based on mutual regard and respect. For the Lady Loyse had adventured, disguised as a blank shield mercenary, into the heart of enemy territory when she and my mother had been ranged against all the might of Kars and Duke Yvian.

Upon her long delayed recovery the Lady Jaelithe assumed once more her duties with my father as vice-warder. Together they had control of the Power, not after the same fashion as the Witches, but in another way. And I know now that the Witches were both jealous and suspicious of the gift so shared, though it was used only for the good of the Old Race and Estcarp. The Wise Ones found such talent unnatural in a man and secretly always reckoned my mother the less because of her uniting with Simon. At this time the Council appeared to have no interest in us children. In fact their attitude might be more termed a deliberate ignoring of our existence. Kaththea was not subjected to examination for inherited Power talent as were all girls of the Old Race before they were six.

I do not remember my mother much from those years. She would descend upon the manor, trailed by fighters from the Border forces—of much greater interest to me, for my first crawl across the floor took me to lay a baby's hand on the polished hilt of a sword. Her visits were very few, my father's even less; they could not often be spared from the patrol along the south border. We turned to Anghart for all answers to childish problems, and held the Lady Loyse in affection. To our mother was given respect and awe, and our father had much the same recognition. He was not a man who was easy with children, I believe, and perhaps he unconsciously held against us the suffering our birth had caused his wife who was the one person he held extremely dear.

If we did not have a closeknit relationship with our parents, we made up for that with a tight bond among the three of us. Yet in nature we were different. As my mother had wished, I was first a warrior, that being my approach to life. Kemoc was a thinker—presented with any problem his was not the response of outright and immediate action, but rather a considered examination and inquiry into its nature. Very early he began his questions, and when he found no one could give him all the answers he wished, he strove to discover the learning which would.

Kaththea felt the deeper. She had a great oneness, not only with us, but things about us—animals, people, even the countryside. Oftentimes her instinct topped my force of action or Kemoc's considered reasoning.

I cannot remember the first time we realized that we, too, possessed a gift of the Power. We need not be together, or even miles close, to be in communication. And when the need was we seemed a single person—I the arms for action, Kemoc the brain, Kaththea the heart and controled emotion. But some wariness kept us from revealing this to

12

those about us. Though I do not doubt that Anghart was well aware of our so-knitted strength.

We were about six when Kemoc and I were given small, specially forged swords, dart guns suited to our child hands, and began the profession of arms which all of the Old Race must follow during this eventide. Our tutor was a Sulcarman, crippled in a sea fight, sent by our father to give us the best training possible. He was a master of most weapons, was Otkell, having been one of Hostovrul's officers during the raid on Kars. Though neither of us took to the use of the axe, to Otkell's disappointment, both Kemoc and I learned other weapon play with a rapidity which pleased our instructor; and he was not in any way easy with us.

It was during the summer of our twelfth year that we rode on our first foray. By that time Pagar had reduced his unruly duchy to order and was prepared once more to try his luck north. The Sulcar fleet was raiding Alizon, his agents must have reported that. So he sent flying columns north through the mountains, in simultaneous clawing attacks at five different places.

The Falconers took out one of these, the Borderers two more. But the remaining two bands made their way into valley land which the enemy had never reached before. Cut off from any retreat they fought like wild beasts, intent on inflicting all the damage they could before they were dragged down.

So it was that a handful of these madmen reached Es River and captured a boat, putting her crew to the sword. They came downstream with some cunning, perhaps in a very vain hope of reaching the sea. But the hunt was up and a warship was in position at the river's mouth to cut them off.

They beached their stolen boat not five miles from Etsford and the whole of the manpower from the farms around turned out in a hunt. Otkell refused to take us along, an order we took in ill part. But the small force he led was not an hour gone when Kaththea intercepted a message. It came so sharply into her mind that she held her head and cried out as she stood between us on the watch walk of the center tower. It was a Witch sending, not aimed at a girl child a few miles away, but for one of the trained Old Race. And a portion of its demand for speedy aid reached us in turn through our sister.

We did not question the rightness of our answer as we rode forth, having to take our horses by stealth. And there was no leaving Kaththea behind—not only was she our directional guide, but we three had become a larger one in that moment on the tower walk.

Three children rode out of Etsford. But we were not ordinary children as we worked our way across country and approached a place where the wild wolves from Karsten had holed up with a captive for bargaining. Battle fortune does exist. We say this captain or that is a "lucky" man, for he loses few men, and is to be found at the right place at the right moment. Some of this is strategy and skill, intelligence and training serving as extra weapons. But other men equally well trained and endowed are never so favored by seeming chance. Battle fortune rode with us that day. For we found the wolves' den, and we picked off the guards there—five of them, all trained and desperate fighters—so that a woman, bloodstained, bound, yet proud and unbending, came out alive.

Her gray robe we knew. But her searching stare, her compelling measurement made us uneasy, and in some manner broke the oneness of our tie. Then I realized that she had dismissed Kemoc and me, that her attention was focused on Kaththea, and by that direct study we were all threatened. And, young as I was, I knew we had no defense against this peril.

Otkell did not allow our breech of discipline to pass, in spite of our success. Kemoc and I bore body smarts which lasted a few days. But we were glad because the Witch was swiftly gone out of our lives again, having spent but a single night at Etsford.

It was only much later, when we had lost the first battle of our personal struggle, that we learned what had followed upon that visit—that the Witches had ordered Kaththea to their testing and that our parents had refused, and that the Council had had to accept that refusal for a time. Though they were not in any way defeated by it. For the Witches never believed in hasty action and were willing to make time their ally.

Time was to serve them so. Simon Tregarth put to sea two years later on a Sulcar ship, his purpose an inspection of certain islands reported newly fortified in a strange way by Alizon. There was a hint of possible Kolder revival there. Neither he nor his ship were heard from again.

Since we had known so little of our father, his loss made small change in our lives—until our mother came to Etsford. This time it was not for a short visit: she came with her personal escort to stay.

She spoke little, looked out overmuch—not on the country, but to that which we could not see. For some months she shut herself up for hours at a time in one of the tower rooms, accompanied by the Lady Loyse. And from such periods the Lady Loyse would emerge whitefaced and stumbling, as if she had been drained of vital energy, while my mother grew thinner, her features sharper, her gaze more abstracted.

Then one day she summoned the three of us into the tower room. There was a gloom in that place, even though three windows were open on a fine summer day. She gestured with a fingertip and curtains fell over two of those windows, as if the fabric obeyed her will, leaving open only that to the north. With a fingertip again she traced certain dimly-seen lines on the floor and they flared into flickering life, making a design. Then, without a word, she motioned us to stand on portions of that pattern while she tossed dried herbs on a small brazier. Smoke curled up and around to hide us each from the other. But in that moment we were instantly one again, as we had ever been when threatened.

Then—it is hard to set this into words that can be understood by those who have not experienced it—we were aimed, sent, as one might shoot a dart or strike with a sword. And in that shooting I lost all sense of time, or distance, or identity. There was a purpose and a will and in that I was swallowed up beyond any protesting.

Afterwards we stood again in that room, facing our mother—no longer a woman abstracted and remote, but alive. She held out her hands to us, and there were tears running down her sunken cheeks.

"As we gave you life," she said, "so have you returned that gift, oh, my children!"

She took a small vial from the table and threw its contents upon the now dying coals in the brazier.

There was a flash of fire and in that moved things. But tht nature of them, or what they did, I could not say. They were gone again and I was blinking, no longer a part, but myself alone.

Now my mother no longer smiled, but was intent. And that intentness was no longer concentrated upon her own concerns, but upon the three of us.

"Thus it must be: I go my way, and you take another road. What I can do, I shall—believe that, my children! It is not the fault of any of us that our destiny is so riven apart. I am going to seek your father—for he still lives—elsewhere. You have another fate before you. Use what is bred in you and it shall be a sword which never breaks nor fails, a shield which will ever cover you. Perhaps, in the end, we shall find our separate roads are one after all. Which would be good fortune past all telling!"

THREE AGAINST THE WITCH WORLD

II

IT WAS thus that our mother rode out of our lives on a hot
midsummer morning when the dust rose in yellow puffs
under the hooves of the mounts and the sky was cloud-
less. We watched her go from the walk on the tower.
Twice she looked back and up, and the last time she
raised her hand in a warrior's salute—to which Kemoc and
I made fitting return in formal fashion, the brilliant sun
mirroring on the blades of our drawn swords. But Kaththea,
between us, shivered as if chill fingers of an out-season wind
touched her. And Kemoc's left hand sought hers, to cover
it where fingers gripped the parapet.

"I saw him," she said, "when she drew upon us in the
search—I saw him—all alone— There were rocks, tall rocks,
and curling water—" This time her shudder shook her whole
thin frame.

"Where?" Kemoc demanded.

Our sister shook her head. "I cannot tell, but it was
far—and more than distance of land and sea lies between."

"Not enough to keep her from the searching," I said as
I sheathed my sword. There was a sense of loss in me,
but who can measure the loss of what one has never
had? My mother and father dwelt inwardly together in a
world they had made their own, unlike most other hus-
bands and wives I had noted. To them that world was
complete and all others were interlopers. There was *no*

17

Power, good or evil, which could hold the Lady Jaelithe from her present quest as long as breath was in her. And had we offered aid in her search, she would have put us aside.

"We are together." Kemoc had picked my thought out of my skull, as was common with us.

"For how long?" Again Kaththea shivered and we turned quickly to her, my hand again to weapon hilt. Kemoc's on her shoulder.

"You mean?" he asked, but I thought that I had the answer.

"Seeresses ride with warriors. You need not remain here when Otkell allows us to join the Borderers!"

"Seeresses!" she repeated with emphasis. Kemoc's hold on her grew tighter, and then I, too, understood.

"The Witches will not take you for training! Our parents forbade it."

"Our parents are no longer here to speak!" Kemoc flung at me.

Then fear claimed us. For the training of a Witch was not like a warrior's daily use of sword, dart gun, or axe. She went away from all those of her blood, to a distant place of mysteries, there to abide for years. When she returned she no longer recognized kin of blood, only kinship with those of her calling. If they took Kaththea from us to become one of their gray robed ranks she might be lost forever. And what Kemoc had said was very true—with Simon and the Lady Jaelithe gone, who remained who could put a strong barrier between our sister and the desires of the Council?

Thus from that hour our life lay under a shadow. And the fear strengthened the bond between us into a tight ring. We knew each other's feelings, though I had less skill than Kemoc and Kaththea. But days passed, and life continued as it always had. Since no fear remains sharp unless it is fed by new alarms, we relaxed.

We did not know then that our mother had wrought for us as best she could before she departed from Estcarp.

THREE AGAINST THE WITCH WORLD

For she went to Koris and had him swear on the Axe of
Volt—that supernatural weapon only he could wield and
which had come to him directly from the dead hand of one
who might be less than a god but who had certainly been
more than human—swear that he would protect us from
the wiles of the Council. Thus he took oath and we lived
at Etsford as always.

Years passed and now the raids from Karsten grew more
continuous. Pagar returned to his old policy of wearing us
down. He met a flat defeat in the spring of the year we
counted seventeen winters behind us, the larger force he
had sent going to their deaths in a pass. And in that battle
Kemoc and I had a part, being numbered among the scouts
who combed the ridges to harry fugitives. We found war
to be a dark and ugly business, but our breed continued
to survive so, and when one has no choice one turns to
the sword.

It was mid-afternoon as we cantered along a trail when
the summons came. Kaththea might have stood before me,
crying out in terror. For though my eyes did not see her,
yet her voice rang not only in my ears, but through my
body. And I heard Kemoc shout, then his mount jostled
mine as I also used spurs.

Our commander was Dermont, an exile from Karsten who
had joined the Borderers when my father first organized that
force. He reined around to front us. There was no expression on his dark face, but so efficiently did he block passage that even our determination was stayed.

"What do you?" he asked.

"We ride," I answered, and I knew that I would cut
down even him, should he hold that barrier of man and
horse against us. "It is a sending—our sister is in danger!"

His gaze searched my eyes, and he read the truth in
what I said. Then he reined to the left, opening the way to
us.

"Ride!" It was both permission and an order.

How much did he know of what chanced? If he was
aware, he did not agree with it. And perchance he was

willing to let us make our try, for, young as we were, we had not been the least of those who had followed him uncomplaining through hard days and weary nights.

Ride we did, twice swapping mounts in camps where we left the impression we rode on orders. Gallop, walk, gallop, doze in the saddle in turns during the walking. A haze of time passed—too much time. Then Etsford was a shadow in a wide expanse of fields where grain had been lately harvested. What we had feared most was not to be seen—there was no sign of raiders. Fire and sword had not bitten here. Yet we had no lightening of our burden.

Dimly, through the ringing in my ears, I heard the horn alert of the tower watchman as we spurred down the road, urging our weary mounts to a last burst of speed. We were white with dust but the House badge on the breasts of our surcoats could be read, and we had passed the spell barrier with no hurt, so they would know we were friends.

My horse stumbled as we came into the court and I struggled to free my stiff feet from the stirrups and dismount before he went to his knees. Kemoc was a little before me, already staggering on his two feet to the door of the Hall.

She was standing there, her two hands bracing her strong body so that she met us on her feet by one last effort of will. Not Kaththea, but Anghart. And at the look in her eyes Kemoc wavered to a halt, so that I charged into him, and we held to one another. My brother spoke first:

"She is gone—they have taken her!"

Anghart nodded—very slowly, as if the motion of her head was almost too hard an effort. Her long braids fell forward, their brown now heavily streaked with white. And her face!—she was an old woman, and a broken one, from whom all will to live had been torn. For torn it had been. This was a stroke of the Power; in that instant we both recognized it. Anghart had stood between her nursling and the will of a Witch, pitting her unaided human strength and energy against a force greater than any material weapon.

"She—is—gone—" Her words were without inflection, gray ghosts of speech from the mouth of death. "They have set a wall about her. To ride after—is—death."

We did not want to believe, but belief was forced upon us. The Witches had taken our sister and shut her off from us by a force which would kill spirit and body together, should we follow. Our deaths could avail Kaththea nothing. Kemoc clutched at my arm until his nails bit into my skin. I wanted to beat back at him, smash flesh and bone—tear —rend— Perhaps the physical weakness left from our long ride was our salvation at that moment. For when Kemoc flung his arm across his face with a terrible cry and collapsed against me, his weight bore us both to the ground.

Anghart died within the hour. I think that she had held on to life with her two hands because she waited for us. But before her spirit went forth, she spoke to us again, and, the first shock being past, those words had meaning and a certain small comfort for us.

"You are warriors." Her eyes went from Kemoc to me and then back to my brother's white and misery-ravaged face. "Those Wise Ones think of warriors only as force of action. They disdain them at heart. Now they will expect a storming of their gates for our dear one. But—give them outward acceptance now and they will, in time, believe in it."

"And in the meantime," Kemoc said bitterly, "they will work upon her, fashioning from Kaththea one of their nameless Women of Power!"

Anghart frowned. "Do you hold your sister so low, then? She is no small maid to be molded easily into their pattern. I think that these Witches shall find her far more than they expect, perhaps to their undoing. But this is not the hour—when they are expecting trouble—to give it to them."

There is this about warrior training: it gives one a measure of control. And since we had always looked to Anghart for wisdom from our childhood, we accepted what she told us now. But, though we accepted, we neither forgot nor forgave. In those hours we cut the remaining bonds which tied us in personal allegiance to the Council.

If at that moment it seemed lesser, there was more ill news. Koris of Gorm, he who had been all these years to most of Estcarp an indestructable buttress and support, lay in the south sorely wounded. To him had gone the Lady Loyse, thus opening the door for Kaththea's taking. So all the safe supports which had based our own small world were at once swept away.

"What do we now?" Kemoc asked of me in the night hours when we had taken Anghart to her last bed of all, and then sat together in a shadow-cornered room, eating of food which had no taste.

"We go back—"

"To the troop? To defend those who have done this thing?"

"Something of that, but more of this, in the eyes of all we are green youths. As Anghart said, they will expect us to engage in some rash action and that they will be prepared to counter. But—"

His eyes were now agleam. "Do not say of yourself again, brother, that you do not think deeply. You are right, very right! We are but children in their eyes, and good children accept the dictates of their elders. So we play that role. Also—" He hesitated and then continued, "There is this— we can learn more of this trade they have bred us to— this use of arms against a pressing enemy—and in addition seek learning in other directions—"

"If you mean the Power, we are men, and they hold it is for the use of women only."

"True enough. But there is more than one kind of Power. Did our father not have his own version of it? The Witches could not deny that, though they would have liked to. All knowledge is not bound up in their own tight little package. Have you not heard of Lormt?"

At first the name meant nothing to me. And then I recalled a half-heard conversation between Dermont and one

22

of the men who had been with him since he had fled Karsten. Lormt—a repository of records, ancient chronicles.

"But what have we to learn from the records of old families?"

Kemoc smiled. "There may be other material there of service to us. Kyllan," he spoke sharply, as one giving an order, "think of the east!"

I blinked. His command was foolish. East—what was east? —why should I think of the east? East—east—I hunched my shoulders, alerted by an odd tingle along the nerves. East— There was the north where lay Alizon ready to spring at our throats, and south where Karsten now worried our flanks, and west where lay the ocean roamed by Sulcar ships, with any number of islands and unknown lands beyond the horizon's rim, such as the land where Simon and Jaelithe had found the true Kolder nest. But to the east there was only a blank—nothing at all—

"And tell me the why of that!" Kemoc demanded. "This land has an eastern border too, but have you ever heard any speech of it? Think, now—what lies to the east?"

I closed my eyes to picture a map of Estcarp as I had seen it many times in use in the field. Mountains—?

"Mountains?" I repeated hesitantly.

"And beyond those?"

"Only mountains, on every map—nothing else!" I was certain now.

"Why?"

Why? He was very right. We had maps showing far north, far south, beyond our boundaries, in every detail. We had ocean charts drawn by the Sulcar. We had nothing —nothing at all for the east. And that very absense of fact was noteworthy.

"They cannot even think of the east," Kemoc continued.

"What!"

"It is very true. Question anyone, over a map, of the east. They cannot discuss it."

"*Will* not, maybe, but—"

23

"No." Kemoc was definite. "*Cannot*. They are mindblocked against the east. I am ready to swear to that."

"Then—but why?"

"That we must learn. Do you not see, Kyllan, we cannot stay in Estcarp—not if we free Kaththea. The Witches will never allow her out of their hold willingly. And where could we go? Alizon or Karsten would welcome us—as prisoners. The House of Tregarth is too well known. And the Sulcarmen would not aid us when the Witches were our enemies. But suppose we vanish into a country or place they refuse to admit has existence—"

"Yes!"

But it was so perfect an answer that I mistrusted it. Behind the smiling face of fortune often hides the cracked countenance of ill luck.

"If there is a block in their minds, there is a reason for it, a very good one."

"Which I do not deny. It is up to us to discover what it is, and why, and if it can be turned to our purpose."

"But if them, why not us—?" I began, and then answered my question with another: "Because of our half-blood?"

"I think so. Let us go to Lormt and perhaps we'll have more than one explanation."

I got to my feet. Suddenly the need to do something, for positive action, was pain to me. "And how do we manage that? Do you suppose that the Council will allow us to roam about Estcarp under the circumstances? I thought you had agreed that we should be obedient, return to the company, act as if we acknowledged defeat."

Kemoc sighed. "Do you not find it hard to be young, brother?" he asked. "Of course we shall be watched. We do not know how much they suspect that we are bound to Kaththea in thought contact. Surely our bolting here at her message will tell them something of that. I—I have not reached her since." He did not look to me to see if I could give a different report. It had never been put into words with us but we all knew that between Kemoc and Kaththea

24

the communication ties were far more secure; it was as if the time gap between our births had set me a little apart from the other two.

"Kemoc—the tower room! Where our mother—" Remembrance of that time when I had been a part of a questing was not good, but I would will myself into that joyfully if it would avail us now. Only he was already shaking his head.

"Our mother was an adept, with years of use of the full Power behind her. We have not the skill, the knowledge, the strength for that road, not now. But what, we have we shall build upon. As for Lormt—well, I believe that willing can also open gates. Perhaps not yet—but there will be a road to Lormt for us."

Was it a flash of foreknowledge which made me correct him?

"For you. Lormt is yours, I am sure, Kemoc."

We did not tarry at Etsford; there was nothing any longer to hold us. Otkell had commanded the small force to escort the Lady Loyse to South Keep. And not one among the handful of retainers left there had the authority or reason to stay us when we announced our return to our company. But as we rode the next day we were at work inwardly—striving to communicate, to speak by thought, with a determination we had never really given to such exercises before. Without guidance or training we struggled to strengthen what talent we had.

And during the months which followed we kept at that task which was hidden from our camp fellows. But hide it we were sure we must. No effort on our part ever awoke a response from Kaththea, though we were informed that she had entered the completely cloistered dwelling of the novices of the Power.

Some side issues of our talent did manifest themselves. Kemoc discovered that his will, applied to learning, could implant much in his memory from a single listening, or sighting, and that he might pick out of other minds such information. The questioning of prisoners was increasingly

25

FAIRHOPE PUBLIC LIBRARY
10 N. Summit St.
Fairhope, AL 36532

left to him. Dermont may have guessed the reason for Kemoc's success in that direction, but he did not comment upon it.

While I had no such contribution to make to our mountain missions, I was aware, slowly, of another reach of whatever lay within me that was an inheritance from my parents. And this took the form of kinship with animals. Horses I knew probably as no other warrior of the forces. The wild things of the wilderness I could draw to me, or send on their way merely by concentrating upon them. The mastery of horses I put to good use, but the other was not a matter of much moment.

As to Kemoc's desire to get to Lormt, there seemed to be no way to achieve that. The scrimmages along the border grew in intensity and we were absorbed into the guerrilla tactics. As the outlook for Estcarp grew darker we were all aware that it was only a matter of time before we would be fugitives in an overrun land. Koris did not recover swiftly from his wounding, and when he did, he was a maimed man, unable to again raise Volt's Axe. We heard the story of how he made a mysterious trip into the sea cliffs of the south and returned thereafter without his super weapon. From that moment his luck was left behind also, and his men suffered one defeat upon the heels of another.

For months Pagar played with us, as if he did not want to quite deliver the finishing blow, but amused himself in this feinting. There was talk of Sulcar ships departing with some of the Old Race aboard. Yet I am sure that what really delayed the final push of our enemies was their age-old fear of the Power and what might chance should the Witches loose on them all that might be so aimed. For no one, even among us, *knew* exactly what the Power might do if a whole nation of Witches willed it into action. It might burn out Estcarp, but it could also take with it the rest of our world.

It was at the beginning of the second year after Kaththea was taken that the road to Lormt opened for Kemoc, but not in a fashion we would have wished. He was trapped in an ambush and his right hand and arm so mangled that it would be long before he could freely use them, if ever he did again. As we sat together before they took him away for treatment we had our last words together:

"Healing is fast, if willed. And add your will to mine, Brother," he told me briskly, though his eyes were pain shadowed. "I shall heal as swiftly as I can, and then—"

He need put no more into words.

"Time may turn against us," I warned him. "Karsten can press home at any time. Do we have even hours left?"

"I will not think of that. What I do, you shall know! I cannot believe that this chance shall be denied us!"

I was not alone as I had feared I might be when Kemoc was borne off slung in a horse litter. We had wrought well, for he was in my mind, even as I was in his. And the distance between us only thinned that bond a little, making us expend more effort. I knew when he went to Lormt. Then he warned me that we must cut contact, unless the need was great, for at Lormt he found or detected influences which tasted of the Power and these he thought perhaps a danger.

Then—for months—silence.

Still I rode with the Borderers, and now, young as I was, I headed my own small command. Uniting us was a comradship forged of danger, and I had my friends. But still I always knew that that other bond was the stronger, and, should either Kaththea or Kemoc summon, I would be a-horse and gone, uncaring. Fearing just that, I began to train my own replacement and did not allow myself to become too involved in any matter beyond my regular duties. I fought, skulked, waited . . . and it seemed that the waiting was sometimes longer than my endurance.

III

WE WERE as lean and vicious as those hounds the Riders of Alizon train for the hunting of men, and, like those fleet beasts, we coursed through the narrow valleys and over mountains, faintly surprised each night that we still sat the saddle or tramped the narrow trails of the heights, and again in the morning when we awoke in our concealed camps, able to greet the dawn alive.

If Alizon and Karsten had made common cause, as all these years we had looked to them to do, Estcarp would have been cracked, crunched, and swallowed up. But it would seem that Pagar had no wish to drink cup-brotherhood with Facellian of Alizon—the why might stem from many causes. Perhaps the heart of those was some use of the Power which we did not detect. For we *did* know that the Witches of the Council had their own way of dealing with a few men, whereas the Power weakened and lost control when it was spread too thin, or when it was put to a prolonged use. For such an effort needed the life force of many adepts working together, and would leave them drained for a perilous space thereafter.

However, it was that very act which they determined upon in the late summer of the second year after Kemoc left us. Orders came by sending to every post, no matter how remote, or how mobile the men who held it. And rumor followed directly behind, as is the way in armies. We were to withdraw, out of the mountains, down from the foothills, gather onto the plains of Estcarp, leaving the ground we had defended so long bare of all who wore Estcarp's badge.

To the outer eye it was the folly of one wit-struck, but rumor had it that we were setting a trap, such a trap as our world had not seen—that the Witches, alarmed at the constant drain of our manpower in these endless engagements, were to concentrate their forces in a gamble which would either teach Pagar a lesson he would never forget, or let us all go down to a single defeat in place of this slow bloodletting.

But we were also ordered to retreat with skulker's skill so that it would be a little time before their raiders would discover that the mountains were empty, the passes free. Thus we flitted back, company by company, squad by squad, with a screen of rear guard behind us. And it was a week or more of redeployment before the Old Race were all in the low lands.

Pagar's men were cautious at first. Too many times had they been slashed in ambushes and attacks. But they scouted, they explored, and then they began to come. A Sulcar fleet gathered in the great bay into which emptied the Es River, some of the ships anchoring even at haunted Gorm, where no man lived unless under orders because of the terror that the Kolders had wrought there, others in the very river mouth. And the tale was that should our present plan fail, the remnants of the Old Race, those who could make it, would be taken aboard that fleet for a last escape by sea.

But that story, we thought, was only for the ears of any spies Alizon and Karsten might have among us. For this move was one born of extreme desperation, and we did not believe the Council were fools. Perhaps the story did bring the Karsten Army at a faster trot via the cleared passes, for they began to pour up into the hills and mountains in an unending river of fighting men.

Chance led my own company to within a few miles of Etsford, and we built our fire and set up a picket line in the later afternoon. The horses were restless, and as I walked among them, striving to sense the reason for their nervousness, I felt it also—a hovering feeling, perhaps not of doom, but of gathering pressure, of a juggling of the balance of nature. So that which was right and proper was now askew, and growing more so by the second, a sucking out of the land and those on it, man and animal, of some inner strength—

An ingathering! Out of nowhere came that thought and I knew it for the truth. That which was the life of Estcarp itself was being drawn in upon some central core—readied—

I reached the horses with what quieting influence I had, but I was very aware now of that sucking. No bird sound broke the oppressive silence, not a leaf or blade of grass moved under any touch of wind, and the heat was a heavy, sullen cover over us. Through that dead calm of waiting, perhaps the more acute because of it, flashed an alert to strike me like a Karstenian dart.

—Kyllan—Etsford—now!

That unspoken summons was the same forceful call for help as the cry from Kaththea had been years earlier. I swung bareback on the horse I held lightly by the mane, jerked free his picket rope. Then I was riding, at a gallop, to the manor which had been our home. There was shouting behind, but I did not look back. I sent a thought ahead:

Kemoc—what is it?

Come! Imperative, no explanation.

The sense of deadening, of withdrawal, held about me as we pounded down the road. Nothing moved in all that land save ourselves, and it was wrong. Yet that wrongness was outside my private concern and I would not yield to it.

There was the watch tower of the manor, but no flag hung limp in the stifling air. I could sight no sentry manning the walk, nor any sign of life about the walls. Then I faced a gate ajar enough to make entrance for a single rider.

THREE AGAINST THE WITCH WORLD

Kemoc awaited me in the door of the hall as Anghart had done on that other day. But he was not Power blasted, half dying; he was vividly alive. So much so that his life force was a fire, battling against the strangeness of the day and hour, so that just looking upon him I was a man who, facing his enemy alone, hears the battle cry of a comrade coming swiftly to share shields. There was no need for speech either of lip or mind. We—how shall I say it?—flowed together in a way past describing, and that which had been cut apart was partially healed. But only partially —for there was that third portion still lacking.

"In time—" He motioned towards the interior of the hall.

I loosed the horse and it trotted for the stable as if a groom were leading it by the reins. Then we were under the roof of Estford once more. It was now an empty place, all those small things which marked daily living gone. I knew that the Lady Loyse now shared quarters with Koris in a border keep. Yet I looked about me, somehow seeking all that had once been ours.

There was a bench by the end of the great table and there Kemoc had put our food, traveler's cakes, and fruit from manor trees. But I did not hunger for that, and for my other hunger I had some appeasement.

"It has been a long time," my brother spoke aloud. "To find a key for such a lock takes searching."

I did not need to ask had he been successful: his triumph shone in his eyes.

"Tonight the Witches make their move against Karsten." Kemoc strode back and forth as if he could not sit still, though I dropped upon the bench, the oppression of the air making me feel even more drained.

"And in three days"—he spun around to face me— "they would set the Witch oath on Kaththea!"

My breath came out in a hiss, not unlike the first battle challenge of one of the high snow cats. This was the point of no return. Either she was brought forth from whatever bonds they had laid upon her before that hour, or she would be absorbed into their whole and lost to us.

"You have a plan." I did not make a question of that. He shrugged. "As good a one as we shall ever have, or so I think. We shall take her forth from the Place of Wisdom and ride—east!"

Simple words, but the action they evoked was another thing. To get a selected one out of the Place of Wisdom was as great a feat as the walking into Kars to bring out Pagar.

As I thought that, Kemoc smiled. He brought up his hand between us. There was a ridge of scar red and rough across its surface and when he tried to flex his fingers, two of them remained stiff and outthrust.

"This was my key to Lormt; I used it well. Also I have used what lies here—to some purpose." He tapped those stiffened fingers against his forehead where the black hair we three shared fell in an unruly curling lock. "There was knowledge at Lormt, very old, veiled in much legend, but I scraped it bare. We shall have such a bolt hole for escape as they will not dream we dare use. As for the Place of Wisdom—"

I smiled then, without humor. "Yes? What is your answer to the safeguards set about that? It will not matter who or what we are, if we are taken within a mile of that without authorization. And it is said that the guards employed are not men to be countered with any weapon we know."

"Do not be too sure of that, brother. The guards may not be men—in that, I believe you speak the truth. But neither are we weaponless. And tomorrow those guards may not be as great as they have been in all other years. You know what will happen in the hours of dark tonight?"

"The Council will move to war—"

"Yes, but how? I tell you, they attempt now the greatest use of the Power that has been tried in generations. They return to what they did once before—in the east!"

"In the east? And that?"

"They will make the mountains to walk, and the land itself answer their will. It is their final throw in the battle against extinction."

"But—can they do that?" The Power could create illusions; it could further communication; it could kill—within narrow range. But that it could accomplish what Kemoc suggested, as if he were assured of its success, I did not quite believe.

"They did it once, and they will try again. But to do so they must build up such a reserve of energy as will sap their resources for some time. I would not wonder if some of them die. Perhaps few may live past the in-gathering and channeling of such force. Thus all the guards they have put on their secret places will be drained and we can win past them."

"You say they did this once in the east?"

"Yes." He had gone back to his striding. "The Old Race were not born in Estcarp—they came across the mountains, or from that direction, so many lifetimes ago that there is no true reckoning. They fled some danger there, and behind them the Power raised mountains, altered the land, walled them away. Then there was a block in their minds, nurtured for some generations until it became an integral part of the race. Tell me, have you found anyone who can speak of the east?"

I had never dared.

Since Kemoc's first uncovering of the puzzle, I had never dared press that too strongly among the Borderers, for fear of arousing suspicion. But it was true, no one ever spoke of the east and should I in devious ways lead to that subject they were as blank of thoughts as if that point of the compass had no existence.

"If what they fled was so terrible that they must take such precautions—" I began.

"Dare we face it now? A thousand years or more lies between that time and now. The Old Race are not what they were then. Any fire burns very low and finally to extinction. I know this, that the three of us will be hunted with greater fury than any Karstenian spy or Alizon Rider, more than any Kolder, if any such still live in this time and world. But not one of them will follow us east."

"We are half of the Old Race—can we break this block to take the trail?"

"That we shall not know until we try. But we can think of it and talk of it, as they cannot. Why, I discovered at Lormt that even the keeper of the old archives did not believe those significant legends which existed. He was not aware of scrolls I consulted, even when I had them spread in plain sight."

Kemoc was convincing. And reckless as the plan was, it was the only one. But there were miles between us and the Place of Wisdom; we had better be on our way. I said as much.

"I have five mounts of the Torgian breed," he replied. "Two here and ready, three others hidden for our last lap of the escape."

He mind-read my astonishment and respect, and laughed. "Oh, it took some doing. They were bought separately over a year's time under other names."

"But how could you know this chance would come?"

"I did not. But I believed that we would have some chance, and I was to be ready for it. You are right, brother: it is time to mount and ride—before the lash of the fury the Wise Women raise may snap back at us."

Torgian horses are from the high moors bordering on the secret marshes of Tor. They are noted for both speed and endurance, a coupling of qualities not always found in the same animal. And they are so highly prized that to gather five of them was a feat I had not thought possible for any individual. For most of them were kept under the control of the Seneschal himself. They were not much to look at, being usually dun colored, with dark manes and coats which did not take a gloss no matter how carefully they were groomed. But for heart, stamina and speed they had no match.

Kemoc had them both saddled with those light saddles used by anti-raider patrols along the seashore. But they

were affected by the general eeriness of this night, danc-
ing a little as we swung up, which was not their usual
manner. We walked them out across the courtyard and beyond the wall. The sun was almost down, but the sky it
bannered held a gathering of purple-black clouds in odd
shapes, and these solidified into a threatening band of
duskiness . . . while the land beneath lay in the same
frightening silence.

My brother had left nothing to chance, which included
his having scouted the fastest route. Yet this night even
Torgian horses could not keep a swift pace. It was as if
we rode through knee deep, ever-shifting sand which sucked
each hoof as it was placed, keeping us to a bare trot when
every nerve demanded a full gallop. The clouds which
had overshadowed the sunset thickened into a cover through
which neither star nor moon shone.

And now a weird embellishment was added to the landscape. I had once ridden along the Tor marsh and seen
those eerie lights native to that forbidden country glow and
dim over its mist-ridden surface. Now such wan gleams began to touch here and there about us—on the tip of a
tree branch, the crown of a bush, along a vine wreathing
a wall. The very alienness heightened the general apprehension which strove to overwhelm us.

Our sense of anticipation grew moment by moment. And
the Torgians reacted to it, snorting and rearing. I called
to Kemoc:

"If we force them on now, they will panic!"

I had been trying to hold them under mental control
for the past half mile, but I could do it no longer. We
dropped out of our saddles, and I stood between the two
mounts, one hand on each strong neck, striving with all
I possessed to keep them from bolting. Then Kemoc's mind
joined with mine, giving me added assistance, and the horses, still snorting, their eyes rolling, foam in sticky strings
about their jaws, trembled but stood firm.

While I was so concentrating upon that task I had not
seen beyond, and now I was shocked by a sharp flash of

fire across the sky. There was, in answer, an ominous grumbling unlike any natural thunder I had ever heard before. And it was not born in the sky above, but out of the ground under us, for that shuddered. The horses screamed, but they did not try to bolt. They crowded under my hold even as I clung to them, dimly feeling in that contact an anchor in a world gone mad.

Those wan lights sprinkled here and there flamed higher, sent sharp points of pallid radiance skyward. Again the crack of lightning, a reply from the earth under us. A long moment of utter silence, then fury such as no man could imagine broke over and around us.

The earth heaved in long rolls, as if under its once stable surface waves moved towards the southern highlands. Wind which had been missing all day burst into frantic life, whipping the candled trees and bushes, tearing the air from our nostrils. One could not fight this—one lost his very identity in such an alien storm. We could only endure and hope, very faintly hope, that we could outlast the raving elements of earth, fire, air, and then water. For there was rain—or could you truly name such stinging lashes of water rain?

If the force of that storm drove us nearly witless, what must it have been like in thost heights were it was brought to a climax? Mountains walked that night, lost themselves in vast waves of earth which ate away their sides, changed lowlands to highlands, and reversed the process by quake, slide, every violent action that could be evoked. The barrier formed by nature between Estcarp and Karsten, which we had kept fortified for years, was wrung, squeezed, wrought by a force which was initiated by human will, and once begun there was no altering of that destructive pattern.

Mind to mind, hand to hand, Kemoc and I made one during that terror. Afterwards we could piece together but a little of the night. Truly it was the end of a world—hearing and sight were soon torn from us, touch only remained and we clung to that sense with a fierce intensity, lest,

36

losing it, we might lose all else, including that which made us what we were.

There was an end—though we had not dared to hope there could ever be. Dark as the matted clouds were over us, still there was light, gray as the tree candles, yet it was a light of the day rather than the weird glow of the storm. We still stood on the road, Kemoc and I and the horses, as if we had been frozen so amid the wild breakage of nature. The ground was solid under our feet, and a measure of sanity had returned, so that our minds might crawl slowly out of the hiding holes we had burrowed within ourselves.

Surprisingly, there was little storm wrack about us. A few branches down, the surface of the road wet and shining. As one we looked to the south. There the clouds were still thick, no gray relieved their night black, and now and again I thought I still saw the spark of lightning.

"What—?" Kemoc began, and then shook his head.

We did not question that the Council had used the Power as never before had it been done in Estcarp. I had very little doubt that Pagar was at last stopped. To be caught in the mountains during that!

I smoothed the wet, tangled mane of my mount. He snorted, stamped, waking out of some ill dream. As I got to saddle I could only marvel at our survival, which still seemed a miracle.

Kemoc had also mounted.

This is our hour!

Mind contact seemed proper, as if whatever we attempted now might awaken some of the force not yet exhausted. We gave the Torgians light rein and this time they broke into their normal, country-covering pace. The day lightened and suddenly a bird broke the cloak of silence with a questioning note. All the pressure and drain had vanished; we were freed and the road was before us, with time now our worst enemy.

From the main highway Kemoc swung off along a lesser way, and here the debris of the storm slowed our pace.

But we kept going, speeding up wherever we had an open space.

Whether we went by obscure paths, or whether the whole of Estcarp lay exhausted from shock that day, we did not know. But we saw no one, not even in the fields about the isolated farms. We might have ridden through a deserted country. And thus fortune favored us.

At nightfall we reached the farmstead with signs of long neglect where we could eat. Turning the Torgians into pasture, we saddled their three fellows Kemoc had left in waiting there. Then we took turns at a quick snatch of sleep. The moon was well up, not blanketed this time, when Kemoc's touch awakened me.

"This is *the* hour," he half-whispered.

And later, as we slid from the saddles and looked down into a hollow where a grove surrounded an age darkened building, he did not have to add:

"This is the place!"

IV

THE LONGER I studied the building in the cup and its surroundings, the more I was conscious of a strange shifting, a rippling—as if between it and us hung a nearly invisible curtain. Distortion of shadow and light, of which I could not quite be certain, blurred a tree, elongated a bush, made even stone waver and move. Yet in another instant all was clear again.

Kemoc held out his maimed hand and my fingers closed about it. Instantly I was drawn into his mind, with an intensity I had not before known. He launched a probe, straight through all that moon and night-cloaked scene, down into the heart of the Place itself.

There was resistence, a wall as defensive to our attack as might be the stronghold of Es to the prick of a single dart gun. Kemoc withdrew speedily, only to launch for a second time his invisible spear, this time with more force, enough to make me gasp as it drained energy from me in one great gulp.

This time we hit that wall, yes, but we went through it, straight on. And then— It was like throwing a very dry branch on a fire—a blaze, fierce, welcoming, rejoicing, feeding—Kaththea! If I had ever faintly believed during the hours we had been riding that she might be changed, that perhaps she would not welcome our interference— I need not have. This was recognition, welcome, a wild desire to be free, all in one. Then, after that first moment of reply, swift apprehension and warning.

She could not give us any accurate idea of which lay between us, other than what we could see for ourselves. But that there were guards, and not human warriors, she knew. Also she dared not move to meet us, and warned off any contact by mind, lest those warders be alarms. Thus she abruptly broke our thread of communication.

"So be it," Kemoc said softly.

I broke his hold, my hand reaching for sword hilt. Yet I knew that steel would have no part in any fight we faced this night.

"To the left, passing under the trees, then a quick run for the wall at that point—" My scouting knowledge took over, seeing each feature of that oddly fluid ground which could be put to our use.

"Yes...."

Kemoc allowed me the lead, deferring to my scout craft. But he was no tyro at this game either, and we flitted

39

down the slope with all the skill we could summon. I discovered that to glance ahead quickly and then away after a single second or so of regard cleared my sight, made that wavering less distracting.

We reached the edge of the wood and the outer defense of the Place fronted us. It was as if we had run full face into a rampart of glass. To the sight there was nothing, not even anything to touch when I struck out—but we could not stir a step ahead.

"Mind—think it away!" Kemoc said, not as if to me, but in self encouragement.

It was hard to make that switch, from action of body to that of mind. But I willed myself forward, told myself that there was no wall, nothing but the earth, the trees growing out of it, the night—even if that night was nowhere as empty as it seemed.

Slowly we advanced, shoving with our wills against the barrier. I shall always believe that Kemoc was right about the effort of mountain turning exhausting the Power. For suddenly that invisible wall gave way, as a dam might suddenly burst agape before the pressure of a flood force. We went forward a few paces at a stumbling run.

"Only the first—"

I did not need that warning from Kemoc. Any defenses set about this heart center of Power would be the most intricate and best known to the Witches. To cheer when one has made a first small assault into a minor victory would be folly indeed.

There was movement among the trees. Again my hand went to weapon hilt. This was tangible—I could see the glint of moonlight on metal, and hear the footsteps of those who came.

Borderers! Here—? The hawk-crested helmet of a Falconer, the winged one of a Sulcarman, our own smooth caps— And then, where faces showed at all beneath that varied headgear they began to glow palely, making plain the features.

Dermont, Jorth, Nikon—I knew these every one, had

ridden with them, shared shields in hot, quick attacks, lain beside them at countless camp fires. Yet now they all turned to me grim faces set with aversion, loathing, and from them came a wave of hatred and disgust, naming me traitor, back fighter. In me flowered the belief that they were right, that it was fit duty for them to cut me down as I stood, so vile a thing had I become. My hand dropped from my sword and I wanted to kneel before them in the dust and—

Kyllan!

Through the wave of guilt and shame rising to drown me that cry cut as might the bow of a serpent ship. Logic and reason battled emotion. They were *not* there, all these comrades-in-arms, judging me to my death. And I was not what they judged me. Though the belief was a smothering weight, I fought it, again willing it away with the same determination as that with which I had fought the invisible wall.

Dermont was before me. The glitter in his eyes was righteous rage, and his dart gun was aimed straight at my throat. But—Dermont was *not* there—he had no place —he was rightfully a tree, a bush, distorted by my own mind which the Power turned against me. I saw the small jerk of his gun as he fired. He *was not* there!

There was no prick of dart—no line of men—no shine of moon on metal! I heard a small, smothered sound from Kemoc.

"So passes their second defense." But his voice was as shaken as I felt.

We went on. I wondered how those guardians had known enough of us to front me with the phantoms of just those men. Then Kemoc laughed, startling me to hear it in that time and place.

"Do you not see, Brother?" He had picked the question out of my mind to answer in words. "They merely supply the impulse, you the actors for its carrying out."

I was irritated that I had not realized that as quickly as he. Hallucinations were the stock in trade of the Witches, and hallucinations grow from seed in a man's own brain.

41

We were under the real walls, honest stone; we could touch and feel the darkness. I wondered at the fact that there had been no more assaults against us.

"They cannot be so easily conquered."

Again Kemoc laughed. "I knew you would not underrate them, Kyllan. The worst should still lie before us."

I stood face against the wall while Kemoc mounted my shoulder and climbed to the top. Then with a hand hold and a pull from his cloak I joined him. We crouched there, looking down into a garden. One side was the wall on which we balanced, the other three sides the building. There was a stillness here, too, a waiting. Yet in the moonlight we could see that the garden was a very fair one.

A fountain played, with small musical sounds, to feed an oval pool, and the fragrance of flowers and scented herbs arose about us. Scent—my mind caught at that: there were herbs the aroma of which could stupefy or drug a man, leaving him open to control by another's desire. I was wary of those flowers.

"I do not think so." Again Kemoc answered my thought. "This is their own dwelling, where they train for the Power. They dare not, for their own safety, play such tricks here." Deliberately he bent his head, drawing in deep breaths, as if testing.

"No—that we do not have to fear." He dropped to the ground and I followed, willing at this time to take such reassurance. But where in that dark bulk of building could we find Kaththea, without arousing all who dwelt there?

"Could we summon her?"

"No!" Kemoc's voice crackled with anger. "No summonings here—they would know of it instantly. That, too, is one of their tools, and they would react to it."

But he seemed as uncertain of the next move as was I. There was the building, utterly dark. And it held rooms we could not number, nor dared we explore them. Now—

Movement again, a shadow which was lighter than the pool of dark marking a door across from which we stood. I froze in an old night fighting trick, using immobility for a type of concealment. Someone was coming into the garden, walking with quiet assurance, obviously not expecting any trouble.

Only great good fortune kept me from speech as she moved into the open moonlight. Dark hair, lying in long, loose strands about her shoulders, her face upraised to the light as if she wished her features clearly seen. A girl's face, yet older, marked now by experience such as she had not known when last I had seen her. Kaththea had solved our riddle—she was coming to meet us!

Kemoc started forward, his hands outstretched. It was my turn to know—to guess— I caught him back. All my scout's instincts rebelled against this smooth solution. Dermont I had seen, and now Kaththea—and she might be no more true than that other. Was she not in our minds, to be easily summoned out?

She smiled and her beauty was such as to catch a man's heart. Slender, tall, her silken black hair in vivid contrast to her pale skin, her body moving with the grace of one who makes walking a formal dance. She held out her hands, her eyes alight, her welcome so plain and warm.

Kemoc pushed at my hold. He did not look at me; his attention was all hers.

"Kemoc!" Her voice was very low, hardly more than a whisper, singing in welcome, longing, joy. . . .

Yet still I held him fast, and he swung in my hold, his eyes angry.

"Kaththea! Let me go Kyllan!"

"Kaththea—perhaps." I do not know what guiding prudence held me to that small particle of disbelief. But either he did not hear, or did not wish to understand.

She was close now, and flowers bent their heads as the hem of her gray robe brushed them. But so had I heard the jingle of metal and the sound of footsteps that were not back in the woods. How could I provide a test which would prove this mirage or truth?

"Kemoc—" Again that half whisper. Yet I was here also. Always there had been that tighter bond between the two

43

of them, yet now her eyes were only for him, she spoke only his name—she did not seem to see me. Why?

"Kaththea?" Suiting my own voice to her low tone, I made her name into a question.

Her eyes did not falter; she never looked to me nor seemed to know I was there. At that moment Kemoc twisted out of my grip, and his went out to catch hers, pulling her to him in a quick embrace. Over his shoulder her eyes looked into mine, still unseeing, and her lips curved in the same set smile.

My questioning had become certainty. If this was a woman and not hallucination, she was playing a game. Yet when we had sought my sister by mind she had been welcoming. And I could not believe that the emotion we had met in that brief contact had been a lie. Could one lie with thoughts? I was sure I could not, though what the Witches might be able to accomplish I had no idea.

"Come!" His arm about her waist Kemoc was pushing her before him toward the wall. I moved—this might be a mistake, but better to learn now when we could retrive our errors.

"Kemoc, listen!" My grip on his shoulder was no light one this time, and I had the greater strength, which I was willing to use.

He struggled for his freedom, dropping his hold on the girl. And his anger was growing with a rapidity which was not normal.

"I do not think this is Kaththea" I said slowly, with all the emphasis I could give to my words. And she just stood there, still smiling, her attention on him as if I were invisible.

"Kemoc—" His name with the same inflection, no word of protest to me.

"You are mad!" my brother's face was white with anger. He was as a man bewitched.

Bewitched! Could I reach him with sense now—in time? I brought his arm up behind his back in a lock and held him so, then pulled him around to face the smiling girl.

44

So holding him in spite of his struggles, I spoke again into his ear.

"Look at her, man! Look at her very well!"

He could not free himself, and look he did. Slowly he stopped struggling, and I hoped my fight won. Kaththea, smiling, undisturbed, now and again uttering his name as if she had only that one word to speak.

"What—what is she?"

I loosed him when he asked that. He knew now, was ready to accept the truth. But what *was* the truth? At our discovery she had not vanished away as had the warriors. I touched her arm—that was flesh beneath my fingers, warm, apparently living. So real a hallucination was beyond any I had seen before.

"I do not know what she is—save she is not who we seek here."

"If we had taken her and gone—" Kemoc paused.

"Yes. That would have served their purposes very well. But if this is counterfiet, where is the real?"

It was as if Kemoc had been shocked into inspired thinking by the closeness of his error.

"This—this one came from there." He pointed to the doorway. "Thus in the opposite direction lies, I think, what we seek."

He sounded too sure, yet I had no better reason or direction in which to look.

"Kemoc—" Her hands were out again. She was watching him and edging to the wall, subtly urging him to that way of escape.

He shivered, drew away. "Kyllan, hurry—we have to hurry!"

Turning his back on her, my brother ran towards the building, and I followed, fearing that any moment a cry of alarm would be voiced behind us, that the surrogate for our sister would utter a warning.

There was another door, and Kemoc, a little before me, put his hand to it. I expected bolts or bars and wondered how we could deal with such. But the panel swung inward readily enough and Kemoc peered into the dark. "Hold to my belt," he ordered. And there was such certainty in his voice that I obeyed. So linked, we moved into a dark which was complete.

Yet Kemoc walked with quick, sure steps, as if he could see every foot of the way. My shoulder brushed against the side of another doorway. Kemoc turned to the left. I felt about with my other hand, touched a surface not too far away, and ran fingertips along it as we moved. A hallway, I thought.

Then Kemoc halted, turned sharply to the right, and there was the sound of another door opening. Sudden light, gray and dim, but light. We stood on the threshold of a small, cell-like room, I looking over Kemoc's shoulder. On the edge of a narrow bed she sat, waiting for us.

There was none of the serene, smiling, untroubled beauty that the girl in the garden had worn. Experience showed on this girl's face also, but with it anxiety, strain, a wearing down of the body by the spirit. Beauty, too, but a beauty which was worn unconsciously and not as a weapon. Her lips parted, formed two names silently. Then Kaththea was on her feet, running to us, a hand for each.

"Haste, oh, haste!" Her voice was the thinnest of whispers. "We have so little time!"

This time there was no need for warning. I had Kaththea in my arms, no simulacrum of my sister. Then she crowded past us and took the lead back through the dark, drawing us with her at a run. We burst into the free night of the garden. I half expected Kaththea to meet her double, but there was no one there.

Back over the wall and into the wood we went, her frantic haste now spurring us. She held the long skirts of her robe high, dragging them with sharp jerks from the bushes where they appeared to catch and hold unnaturally. We strove not to use care now, only speed. And we were all gasping as we came out of the hollow to where our Torgians waited.

Just as we reached the saddles a deep boom welled

from the building in the cup. It held a little of the earth-thunder we had heard during the mountain moving. Our horses screamed shrilly, as if they feared another such upheaval of their normal world. As we started off at a wild gallop I listened for any other sounds—shouts of some pursuit, another thunder roar. But there was nothing.

Not in the least reassured, I called to Kaththea:

"What will they send after us?"

Her hair whipped back, her face a white oval, she turned to answer me. "Not—warriors—" she gasped. "They have other servants—but tonight—they are limited."

Even Torgians could not stand the pace we had set in fleeing the valley of the Place. I was aware that the horses were disturbed, and that this uneasiness was fast approaching panic. Yet the reason for that was not plain since we should be out of the influence of the Place by now. With all the talent I had I strove to quiet their minds, to bring them again to sane balance.

"Rein in!" I ordered. "They will run themselves blind—rein in!"

I had no fears for Kemoc's horsemanship. But of Kaththea's I was not so sure. While the Witches did not ignore the body in their training and exploration of the mind, I did not know how cloistered my sister had been during these past years, how able to control her mount.

The Torgians fought for the bits, strove to continue their headlong run, but between our strength on the reins, and my own efforts, they began to yield and we were slowing our pace when there was an ear-splitting squawl from before us. The cry of a snow cat, once heard, is never to be mistaken. They are the undisputed kings of the high valleys and the peaks. Though what one could be doing this far from its native hunting grounds, I did not understand. Unless the orders which had brought us from the border lands had been accompanied by some unknown commands which had moved the animals also, spreading them into territory they had not known before.

My mount reared and screamed, lashing out with front

hooves as if the cat had materialized beneath its nose. And Kemoc fought a like battle. But the Torgian my sister rode swung about and bolted the way we had come, at the same breakneck pace which had started us off on this wild ride. I spurred after her, striving to reach the mind of her mount, with no effect, since it was now filled with witless terror. All I could read there was that it imagined the snow cat behind it preparing for a fatal leap to bring it down.

My horse fought me, but I drove savagely into its brain and did what I had never presumed to do before—I took over, pressing my wishes so deeply that nothing was left of its own identity for the present. We caught up with Kaththea and I stretched my control to the other horse—not with such success, since I also had to hold my own, but enough to eject from its brain the fear of imminent cat attack.

We turned to see Kemoc pounding up through the moonlight. I spoke between set teeth:

"We may not be able to keep the horses!"

"Was that an attack?" Kemoc demanded.

"I think so. Let us ride while we can."

Ride we did through the waning hours of the night, Kemoc in the lead over the trail he had long ago marked. I brought up the rear, trying to keep ever alert to any new onslaught against our mounts or us. I ached with the weariness of the double strain, I who had believed myself fine trained to the peak of endurance, such as only the fighting men of these later days of Estcarp were called upon to face. Kaththea rode in silence, yet she was ever a source of sustenance to us both.

V

THERE WAS light ahead—could that mark dawn? But dawn was not red and yellow, did not flicker and reach—

Fire! A line of fire across our path. Kemoc drew rein and Kaththea pulled level with him, and a moment later I brought up beside them. That ominous line ahead stretched across our way as far as the eye could see. Under us the horses were restive again, snorting, flinging up their heads. To force them into that would not be possible.

Kaththea's head turned slowly from left to right, her eyes surveying the fire as if seeking some gate. Then she made a small sound, close to laughter.

"Do they deem me so poor a thing?" she demanded, not of us, but of the night shadows before her. "I cannot believe that—or this."

"Illusion?" asked Kemoc.

If it were an illusion it was a very realistic one. I could smell the smoke, hear the crackle of flames. But my sister nodded. Now she looked to me.

"You have a fire striker—make me a torch."

I dared not dismount, lest my Torgian break and run. It was hard to hold him to a stand, but I urged him to the left and leaned in the saddle to jerk at a spindly bush, which luckily yielded to my pull. Thrusting this into Kemoc's hold, I fumbled one-handedly at my belt pouch, dragging forth the snapper to give a fire-starting spark.

The vegetation did not want to catch, but persistence

won and finally a line of flame smoldered sullenly. Kaththea took the bunch of burning twigs and whirled it through the air until the fire was well alight. Then she put her horse forward. Again it was my will which sent the animal in. Kaththea's strange weapon was flung out and away, falling well ahead of us, to catch, so that a second fire spread from it.

They were burning towards each other, as if some magnetism existed pulling them into union. But as the first line reached the one my sister had kindled—it was gone! There remained only the now smoldering swath from the torch lighting. Kaththea laughed again, and this time there was real amusement in the sound.

"Play of children!" she called. "Can you not bring better to front us, ones of great wisdom?"

Kemoc gave a quick exclamation and rode to her, his crooked hand out.

"Do not provoke!" he ordered. "We have been very lucky."

As she looked to him, and beyond to me, her eyes were shining. She had an otherness in her face which put a curtain between us.

"You do not understand," she replied almost coldly. "It is best that we _ face—now—the worst they can summon up against us, rather than later when their power has strengthened and we are wearied. Thus it is well to challenge them, and not wait to do battle when *they* wish!"

Her words made sense to me. But I think that Kemoc still thought this unnecessary recklessness. And for that reason, I, too, began to wonder. For it could well be that our sister, out of her prison, might find freedom so fine a draft that she was not steady in her thinking.

She turned her head a small space farther, giving me her full attention.

"No, Kyllan, I am not drunk with freedom as a six-months Sulcar sailor greets wine the first hour off ship's decking! Though I could well be. Give me this much credit: I know well those I have lived among. We could not have done this thing tonight had they not lost much of their strength through the sending to the mountains. I would meet their worst before they recover—lest they crush us later. So—"

She began to chant, dropping the reins to free her hands for the making of gestures. And oddly enough the Torgian stood rock still under her as if no longer a creature of flesh and bone. The words were very old. Now and again I caught one which had some meaning, a far-off ancestor of one in daily use, but the majority of them were as a tongue foreign to me.

Her words might be foreign but the sense behind them had meaning. I have waited out the suspense of ambush, the lurking fore-terror of a stealthy advance into enemy-held territory, wherein each rock can give hiding place to death. I knew of old that prickle along the spine, that chill of nerve. Where I had met that with action, now I had to sit, waiting only for the doing—of what, I did not know. And I found this much harder than any such wait before.

Kaththea was challenging the Power itself, summoning up some counter-force of her own to draw it like a magnet, as her real fire had drawn that of illusion. But could she triumph now? All my respect and awe of the Witches' abilities argued that she could not. I waited, tense, for the very world to erupt around us.

But what came in answer to my sister's chant was no ground-twisting blow, no hallucination or illusion. It had no visible presence, no outward manifestation. It was—anger. Black, terrible anger—an emotion which was in itself a weapon to batter the mind, crush all identity beneath its icy weight.

Kyllan—Kemoc!

Sluggishly I answered that call to contact. We were not one, but three that had become one. Clumsily perhaps, not too smooth-fitting in our union, yet we were one—to stand against how many? But with that uniting came also Kaththea's assurance. We did not need to attack; our only purpose was defense. If we could hold, and hold, and con-

51

tinue to hold, we had a chance of winning. It was like one of the wrestling bouts in the camps wherein a man sets the whole of his strength against that of another.

I lost all knowledge of myself, Kyllan Tregarth, Captain of Scouts, seated ahorse in the night in a fire scorched clearing. I was no one—only something. Then, through that which was iron endurance, came a message:

Relax.

Without question I obeyed. The answering pressure came down—flat, hard, crushing—

Unite—hold!

We almost failed. But as a wrestler could use an unorthodox move to unsteady his opponent, so had my sister chosen the time and the maneuver. We threw the enemy off balance, even as she had hoped. The crushing descent met once more a sturdy resistance. Its steady push broke a little, wavered. Then came battering blows, one after another, but even I could sense that each one was slower, less strong. At last they came no more.

We glanced from one to the other, again ourselves, three in three bodies, not one in a place where bodies were naught.

Kemoc spoke first: "For a space—"

Kaththea nodded. "For a space—and how long I do not know. But perhaps we have won enough time."

True morning was graying the sky as we rode. But the Torgians were no longer fresh, and we dared not push the pace. We ate in the saddle, the journey bread of the army. And we did not talk much, saving all energy for what might lie ahead.

There were the eastern mountains making a great ridge against the sky, dark and threatening. And I knew that, miles distant though they were, these were the final wall between Estcarp and the unknown. What lay behind them? From all that Kemoc had learned in Lormt, there had once been some danger past all our present reckoning. Was he right—had the toll of years lessened that danger? Or were we riding from a peril we did know into danger we did not, and which would be even greater?

THREE AGAINST THE WITCH WORLD

The day wore on. We kept to the cover of wasteland
when we could. In our favor was the fact that here the
farms were very few and far apart. Most of the ground
was abandoned to second growth woodlands. Fewer and
fewer were the signs that man had ever planted his rule
here.

Still the mountains loomed. Even though we plodded
ever towards their foothills we seemed to approach no closer. They might have been fixed on some huge platform
which moved at a speed equal to ours always ahead. I
waited throughout that whole day for another contest of
wills, or some sign the hunt was up behind us. For I did
not really believe that the Power was so exhausted they
could not bring us up short and hold us captive while
they sent their ministers to take us bodily prisoner.

Yet we rode untroubled. We halted to rest the horses,
to take short naps with one always on watch, and we
rode again. And we saw nothing save now and then a
curious animal peering through some screen of bush. It
was wrong, all wrong; every scout instinct belabored me
with that. We would have trouble, we must have trouble—

"There may be this," Kemoc cut into my thoughts, "—
they do not realize that we are not blocked against the
east, so they believe that we ride now into a trap without
an exit—save back into their hands."

That made sense. Yet I dared not wholly accept it. And,
as we camped that night, without fire, on the bank of a
rock strewn, mountain born stream, I still kept watch with
the feeling that I would be easier in my mind if an attack
did come.

"To think so, Kyllan" —that was Kaththea, gazing up
at me from where she knelt at the streamside washing her
face— "is to open you to attack. A man's uncertainty is
a lever they may use to overset him."

"We cannot go without taking precautions," I countered.

"Yes. And thus always they will have a small door open.
But it is a door which we may not close—you are most

53

right, Brother. Tell me, where do you look for any true hiding place?"

With that she surprised me. What had she thought—that we had taken her from the Place only to ride blindly about the countryside with no foreplan?

Kaththea laughed. "No, Kyllan, I do not think so meanly of your intelligence. That you have a plan, I knew from the moment you called to me from outside the walls of the Place. I know it has something to do with these mountains we seek so wearily. But now is the time to tell the what and the why."

"Kemoc has planned it, let him—"

She shook drops of water from her hands and wiped them on sun dried grass from the stream bank. "Then Kemoc must tell me the whole."

As we sat together, chewing on the sustaining but insipid food, he laid before her the whole story of what he had discovered at Lormt. She listened without question until he has done, and then she nodded.

"I can give you this further proof of your mystery, brother. For the past hour, before we reached this spot, I was riding blind—"

"What do you mean?"

She met my eyes gravely. "Just what I said, Kyllan. I rode through a mist. Oh, it was broken now and then—I could make out a tree, a bush, rocks. But for the most part it was a fog."

"But you said nothing!"

"No, because watching the two of you, I knew it must be some form of illusion which did not trouble you." She wrapped the part of cake she still held in its protecting napkin and restored it to saddle bag. "And it was also not born of anything they had unleashed against us. You say we do not have this block about the east because we are of mixed heritage. That is good sense. But it would also seem that my witch training mayhap has produced a measure of it to confuse me. Perhaps had I taken the oath and become wholly one of them I could not pierce it at all."

"What if it gets worse for you?" I blurted out my growing concern.

"Then you shall lead me," she returned tranquilly. "If it is some long ago induced blank-out, I do not believe it will last—except over the barrier itself, through the mountains. But now I also agree with you, Kemoc. They will relax their hunt, for they will confidently believe that we shall be turned back. They do not realize that at least two of us can go clearsighted into their nothingness!"

I could not share her confidence completely, but also I had learned as a Borderer that worry over what might be never added a single second to a man's life, nor changed his future for well or ill. I had not encountered Kaththea's mist, nor had Kemoc. And her explanation for that was reasonable. But could we continue to be so free? Trailing over mountain tracks with impaired vision was a desperate thing.

Kemoc asked a question forming in my own mind. "This mist—of what manner is it? And you say . . . not complete?"

Kaththea shook her head. "No, and sometimes I think it is a matter of will. If I fasten on something which is only a shadow and sharpen my will, I see it the clearer. But that requires a concentration which might work against us."

"How so?" I demanded.

"Because I must listen—"

"Listen?" My head came up and now I strained to hear too.

"Not with ears," she replied quickly, "but with the inner hearing. They are not moving against us now; they are content to wait. But will they remain so the farther we go eastward, when they at last know that we are not contained by their long set boundries? Do not think they will ever give up."

"Has there ever before been one who refused witchhood, I wonder?" Kemoc asked musingly. "The Council must be as startled by your flight as if one of the stones of Es City spoke out against them. But why should they wish to keep you against your will?"

"It is simple enough—I am not of their same pattern. At first they did not push too hard to have me because of that very thing. There were those in the Council who believed I would be a disrupting influence should they strive to make me one with them. Then, as the menace of Karsten grew worse, they were ready to grasp at any promise, no matter how small, of adding in some way to the sum total of the Power. Thus, they would have me to study, to see if through me any new gates might be opened, that the basic amount of their long treasured force be increased. But as long as I would not take the oath, become one with them in a surrendering of self, they could not use me as they wished. Yet I could not delay such a step too long. There was this—" She paused, her eyes dropped to the hands which had rested lazily in her lap. Now those long fingers curled, came together as if protecting something in their cupped palms. "I wanted—some of what they had to offer, that I wanted! Every part of me thirsted for their knowledge, for I knew that I could work wonders also. Then would come to me the thought that if I chose their path, so must I cut away part of my life. Do you think that one who has been three can happily be alone? Thus I turned and dodged, would not answer when they asked of me this thing. And at last came the time when they would risk all against Karsten.

"They spoke plainly to me—to use the Power in a unification of all their selves meant an ending for some. Many would die, did die, burnt out by making of themselves vessels to hold the energy until it could be aimed and loosed. They had to have replacements and no longer would the choice be left to me. And now, with their ranks so depleted, neither will they allow me to go, if they can prevent it. Also—" Now she raised her eyes to look at us directly. "They will deal with you, the both of you, ruthlessly. They always secretly mistrusted and feared our father; I learned that when I was first among them. It is not natural, according to their belief, that a man should hold even a small portion of the Power. And they more than mistrusted our mother for the talent that she built with our father's aid, when by all rights she should have lost her witchship in lying with a man. This they considered an abomination, a thing against all nature. They know you have some gift. After this past night and day, they will be even more certain of that—with good cause to mislike what they have learned. No normal man could have entered the Place, and he certainly could not have won free of it again. Of course, their safeguards there were depleted, yet they were such as would have been death to any male fully of the Old Race. Thus—you are not to be trusted, you are a menace, to be removed!"

"Kaththea, who was the girl, the one in the garden?" Kemoc asked suddenly.

"Girl?"

"You and yet not you," he answered. "I believed in her —would have taken her and gone. Kyllan would not let me. Why?" He turned now to me. "What was it that made you suspect her?"

"No more than a feeling at first. Then—she was like one made for a purpose. She fastened upon you, as if she wished to hold you—"

"She looked like me?" Kaththea asked.

"Very much, save she was too serene. She smiled always. She lacked" —and I knew I had hit upon the truth — "she lacked humanity."

"A simulacrum! Then they *did* expect you, or some attempt to reach me! But it takes long and long to make one of those. I wonder which one of the novices it really was?"

"Shape changing?" Kemoc said.

"Yes. But more intricate, since she was designed to deceive such as you, who had mind contact—or did they know that much of us? Yes, they must have! Oh, that proves it—they must be very sure now that you are the enemy. And I wonder how much longer we have before they realize we are not in any trap, and so move after us?"

To that question we had no answer. But it left us with little peace of mind. The stream tinkled and burbled through the dark, and we could hear the sound of the hobbled Torgians at graze. And we set up watches turn and turn about.

The morning came and this one was clear and bright for Kemoc and me—though Kaththea admitted that the fog was heavy for her, and that she had a disturbing disorientation when we began our ride into the foothills. At last she begged us to tie her to her saddle and lead her mount, as the overwhelming desire to turn back was growing so strong she feared she could not control it.

We, too, had a measure of unease. There was a distortion of sight at times which was like that we had experienced looking down into the valley of the Place. And the sensation of moving into some dark and unpleasant surprise was haunting, but not to the point that it had any effect upon our determination.

But we did as Kaththea asked and at intervals she struggled against the ties we put on her, once crying out that directly before us was sudden death in the form of a deep chasm—though that was not true. Finally she shut her eyes and had us lay a bandage over them, saying that once shut into her own mind in that fashion, she was better able to combat the waves of panic.

The faint trace of road had long since vanished. We went by the easiest riding we could pick through true wilderness. I had lived much among mountains, but the weirdly broken ways we now followed were strange to nature, and I thought I knew the reason. Just as the mountains of the south had been toppled and turned, so, too, had these heights.

It was evening of the second day since we had left the streamside when we reached the end of open ways. Before us now lay heights a determined man might climb on foot, but not on horseback. We faced that fact bleakly.

"Why do you stop?" Kaththea wanted to know.

"The way runs out; there is only climbing ahead."

"Wait!" She leaned down from her saddle. "Loose my hands!"

There was such urgency in that that Kemoc hastened to obey. As if she could see in spite of the blindfold, her fingers moved surely out, touched his brows, slid down to the eyes he blinked shut. For a long moment she held them so before she spoke:

"Turn, face where we must go."

With her touch still on his closed eyes, my brother moved his head slowly to the left, facing the cliff face.

"Yes, oh, yes! Thus I can see it!" There was excitement and relief in Kaththea's voice. "This is the way we must go, then?"

But how could we? Kemoc and I could have done it, though I wondered about his maimed hand. But to take Kaththea bound and blindfolded—that was impossible.

"I do not think you need to take me so," she answered my silent doubts. "Leave me thus for tonight, let me gather all my powers, and then, with the dawn—let us try. There will be an end to the block, of that I am sure."

But her certainty was not mine. Perhaps with the dawn, instead of climbing, we would have to backtrack, to seek out another way up through the tortured debris of this ancient battlefield.

VI

I COULD NOT sleep, though there was need for it in my body—to which my mind would not yield. Finally I slipped from my blanket and went to where Kemoc sat sentry.

"Nothing," he answered my question before it was voiced. "Perhaps we are so far into the debatable land we need not fear pursuit."

"I wish I knew at whose boundary we are," I said. And my eyes were for the heights that we must dare tomorrow.

"Friend or enemy?" In the moonlight his hand moved so there was a glint of light from the grip of the dart gun lying unholstered on his knee.

"And that—" I gestured to the weapon. "We have but two extra belts of darts. Steel may have to serve us in the end."

Kemoc flexed his hand and those stiff fingers did not curl with their fellows. "If you are thinking of this, brother, do not underrate me. I have learned other things besides the lore of Lormt. If a man determines enough he can change one hand for the other. Tomorrow I will belt on a blade for the left hand."

"I have the feeling that what we win beyond will be sword-taken."

"In that you may be very right. But better land sword-taken than what lies behind us now."

I gazed about. The moon was bright, so bright it seemed uncannily so. We were in a valley between two ridges. And Kemoc had his post on a ledge a little more than a man's height above the valley floor. Yet here our sight was restricted as to what lay above us, or farther down the cut of our back trail. And this blindness worried me.

"I want to see from up there," I told him.

In the brightness of the moon I did not fear trouble, the slope being rough enough to afford good hand and toe holds. Once on the crest I looked to the west. We had been climbing all day as we worked our way through the foothills. The tree growth was sparse now and I had a clear sight. With the long seeing lenses from my service belt I searched our back trail.

They were distant, those pricks of light in the night. No effort had been taken to conceal them; rather they had been lit to let us know we were awaited. I counted some twenty fires and smiled wryly. So much did those who sent those waiting sentries respect the three of us. Judging by Borderer practices there must be well over a hundred men so encamped, waiting. How many of them were those with whom Kemoc and I had ridden? Were any drawn from my own small command? Freed from the necessity of southward patrols they could be used thus.

But we were not yet in a trap. I pivoted to study the cliff wall which now fronted us. As far as the glass advanced my own sight north and south there appeared no easier way up. And would those others, back there, remain at the line they had drawn, or come after us?

I dropped to Kemoc's perch.

"So they are there. . . ."

Mind contact passed news swiftly.

"I make it at least a full field company, if we go by fire count. Maybe more."

"It would seem there is a vow we shall be taken. But I doubt if they will sniff this far in after us."

"I could sight no better climbing place."

There was no need to put the rest of my worry into words: he shared it fully already. But now he gave me a short reply.

"Do not believe that she will not climb, Kyllan."

"But if she does so blind?"

"Two of us, the saddle ropes, and mind contact which will give her sight? We may be slow, but we shall go. And you shall fuzz the back trail, Kyllan, even as it has just crossed your mind to do."

I laughed. "Why do we bother with speech? You know my thoughts as I think them—"

He interrupted, his words sober: "Do I? Do you know mine?"

I considered. He was right, at least as far as I was concerned. I had contact, could communicate with him and with Kaththea, but it was a come and go matter and, as I knew, mostly when we were intent upon a mu-

61

tual problem. Unless he willed it, Kemoc's personal thoughts were not mine.

"Nor yours mine," he replied promptly. "We may be one in will when necessary, but still we are three individuals with separate thoughts, separate needs, and perhaps separate fates also."

"That is good!" I said without thinking.

"It could not be otherwise, or we would be as the non-men the Kolder used to do their labor and their fighting—those bodies who obeyed, though mind and spirit were dead. It is enough to open one surface of our thoughts to one another when we must, but for the rest—it is our own."

"Tomorrow, if I blaze our trail up there and keep my mind open, can Kaththea see thus, even if she goes blinded?"

"So is my hope. But this is also the truth, brother, that such an open mind must be held so by will, and this will add to the strain of the climb. I do not think you can do this for long; we shall have to divide it between us. And"—again he flexed his scarred hand in the moonlight —"do not believe that in this either shall I be found wanting. Crooked and stiff as these fingers are, yet my bone and flesh have learned to obey me!"

That I did not doubt either. Kemoc got to his feet, holstering his gun, and I took his place so that he might rest. We had already agreed that Kaththea would not be one of this night's sentries, since it was her task to wrestle with the block her witch training had set upon her.

As I watched, the very brilliance of the vale began to have its effect. There was a kind of dazzlement about the pallid light, akin to the subtle distortion we had noticed earlier, and I was so inwardly warned against any long study. There was that here which could evoke glamourie— the visionary state into which the half-learned in any magic could easily slip, to be lost in their own visions. And I wanted no such ensorcelment.

At length I dropped from Kemoc's ledge and took to active sentry patrol, keeping on my feet, taking care not to look too long at any rock, bush or stretch of ground. Thus I came to where the Torgians browsed. They moved slowly, and a quick reading of their minds showed me a dulling of their kind of thought. Yet undue fatigue would not normally have brought them to such a state. Perhaps the same block which acted upon the Old Race held in small part for their animals also.

We could not take them with us. And still there was a way they could continue to serve us. It did not take me long to strip off their hobbles. Then I saddled them and set on bridle and bit, looping the reins about the saddle horns. As I worked they became more alert.

As I was about to set on them my last commands, there was a stir behind me. I turned, hand going to my gun. Kaththea was in the open, her hands tugging at the band she herself had fastened to blind her eyes after we had eaten our meal. At a last tug that gave way and she stared in my direction as a short-sighted person might peer.

"What—?" I began, then her hand came up in an impatient gesture.

"There is more which can be done to carry through your scheme, brother," she said softly. "Horses should have riders."

"Dummies? Yes, I had thought of that, but the materials for the making of such are lacking."

"For materials there is not much needed to induce illusion."

"But you have no Jewel of Power," I protested. "How can you build one of the strong illusions?"

She was frowning a little. "It may well be that I cannot, but I shall not be sure until I try. Our mother surrendered her Jewel upon her marriage day, yet thereafter she accomplished much without it. Mayhap the Jewel is not quite as much the focus of the Power as the Wise Women will have us believe. Oh, I am very young in their learning as they count such things, but also am I certain that there has been no proper measurement of what *can* be wrought by wish, will and the Power. If one is content to use a tool then one shall never know what one can do without it. Now, here—" She plucked a curled, silvery leaf from a nearby bush. "Lay upon this some hairs from your head, Kyllan—and pluck them from the roots, for they must be living hairs. Also, moisten them with spittle from your mouth."

Her tone summoned obedience. I took off my helm, and my forehead and throat, about which its mail veil had been wreathed, felt naked and chill in the night breeze. I plucked the hair she wished, and the separate threads curled about my fingers, for it had gone unclipped for some time. Then I spat upon the leaf and laid the hair therein, even as Kaththea was doing in another such improvised carrier.

She crossed to Kemoc and awakened him to do likewise. Then she held the three leaves on her palm and walked to the horses. With her right hand she rolled the first leaf and its strange burden into a spill, all the time her lips murmuring sounds I could not make into any real word. The spill she tucked between the knotted reins and the saddle horn, taking great care as to its wedging. And this she did also with the others. Then she stood aside and raised her hands to her mouth as half open fists. Through these trumpets of flesh and bone she sang, first in a low semi-whisper, then louder and louder. And the rhythm of those sounds became a part of me, until I felt them in the beat of my heart, the throb of my pulses. While the brilliance of the moonlight was a flashing glare, its light condensed to where we stood.

Kaththea's song ended abruptly, on a broken note. "Now! Give your commands, brother—send them forth!"

The orders I set in the Torgians' befogged brains sent them moving down the vale, away from us, in the direction of that fire line. And as they so left us I will always believe that I saw the misty forms in those saddles, a swirl of something to form three riders, nor did I wonder who those riders would seem to be.

64

"It would appear, sister, that the half has not been told concerning the powers of Witches," Kemoc commented.

Kaththea swayed and caught at his arm, so that he gave her his support.

"Witchery has its prices." She smiled upon us wanly. "But I believe that this has bought us time—more than just a night. And now we may rest in peace."

We half-carried her between us to the blanket-branch bed we had earlier made her, and, as she lay with closed eyes, Kemoc looked to me. There was no need for a reading of minds between us—to attempt the mountain climb tomorrow was beyond the borders of reasonable risk. If those who tended those watchfires did not advance and Kaththea's magic bought us more time, we need not push.

Dawn found me back on the lookout ridge. The fires still burned, more difficult to see with the coming of light. I searched for the horses. It was a long and anxious moment before my lenses picked them up, moving across an open glade. And I was startled. There were riders in those saddles, and they would truly have deceived me had I been on scout. They would be watching, those others, and they would see their prey returning. How good the illusion would be at close quarters, I could not guess. But for the time we were covered.

Kemoc joined me and we took turns watching the horses, until a fold in the earth concealed them from us. Then we went down to inspect the cliff wall. It was rough enough to promise adequate holds, and not far from the top was a ledge of some depth to afford a resting place. As to what lay beyond its crests we did not know, but neither could we say that we would be faced by something we could not surmount.

For that day we rested in camp, sleeping so deeply in turn that no dreams troubled us. And Kaththea recovered that strength which had been drawn from her in the weaving of the illusion. At the first shadow of night I climbed the ridge again. This time there was no sparkle of watchfires, nor did we sight any later in the night. What this could mean might be either of two things: Kaththea's pain-fully wrought illusions might have provided the waiting company with prisoners for a space—or they had speedily discovered the trickery, struck camp, and were moving on. Yet a most painstaking use of the lenses, studying each bit of cover which might attract a stalking hunt, showed nothing amiss.

"I think they are truly gone," Kaththea said with a confidence I did not altogether share. "But it does not matter. In the morning we shall go also, up and back—there." She pointed to the mountain.

And in the morning we did go. Our provisions, weapons and blankets were made into packs which Kemoc and I shouldered. And roped between us both was Kaththea, her hands free, no weight upon her. She had discarded the eye bandage, but still kept her eyes closed, striving to "see" through mind contact, since she was still in the confusing fog.

It was slow work, that upward pull, and I found it doubly hard when I had to concentrate not only on my own efforts, but as an aid for Kaththea. She showed a surprising dexterity in spite of her self-imposed blindness, never fumbling or missing a hold I pictured in my mind. But when we reached the ledge I was so weak with fatigue I feared it was not in me to pull up the last short way. Kemoc reached across Kaththea as she crouched between us, his hand falling on my shaking knee.

"The rest to me," he stated as one who would not be denied.

Nor could I have fought him for that danger. I was too spent to risk their safety on my own fast failing strength. So from that rest we reversed and my brother took the lead, his face as rigid with concentration as mine must have been. For I discovered my chin stiff, my jaw aching with pressure when I had come to those moments of relaxation.

It was lucky that I had given way to Kemoc, for the last part of that climb was a nightmare. I forced my trem-

66

bling body to the effort, knowing well the danger of pulling back upon the rope and distracting Kaththea. But there
came an end and we were on a space almost wide enough
to be a plateau.

There was a cold wind here which dried our sweat,
chilled us. So we pressed on hurriedly to where two peaks
jutted skyward, a shadowed cleft between them. And when
we entered that slash Kaththea suddenly flung back her
head and opened her eyes, giving a small but joyful cry.
We did not need any words to know that her blindness was
gone.

The cleft we entered intensified the cold of those heights.
Kemoc scuffed a boot toe through a patch of white and I
saw that he had kicked up snow. Yet this was summer
and the heat of the year had weighed heavily on us below. We stopped to undo our packs and bring out the
blankets, pulling them cloakwise about our shoulders. That
helped in a small measure as we came to the end of the
cleft and looked down—into the world of the unknown.

Our first impression was one of stark disbelief. There was
a kind of wrongness about the broken land which receded
down and down from our present perch, into a misty low-
land so hidden we could not tell whether land or water,
or both, lay far below. All I could think of was a piece
of cloth which had been soaked in thin mud and then
twisted by hand before being allowed to dry, so that a
thousand wrinkles ran this way and that without sane
purpose. I had thought that I knew mountain country, but
this cut up land was worse than the foothills we had passed.

Kaththea was breathing deeply, not just as one who
would fill her lungs, but as if she could separate some one
scent from many, and identify it, as a hound or a snow
cat could identify a hunting trace.

"There is that here—" she began, and then hesitated.
"No, I make no judgments. But this land has felt the lash
of a fury which was man-born and not the stroke of nature. Only that was long and long ago, and the destruction

is under mend. Let us get from this place; I do not like my winds ice-tipped."

In one way the broken nature of the descent served us well—for while the finding of the way was time consuming, yet the terrain was so rough here there were natural stairways of rock to be discovered. Since Kaththea was now sure of her sight, we made far better time than we had on the other side of the mountain.

However, the mist which choked the lower lands still curtained them from us, and that did ·not inspire confidence. There was this also: on the other side of the mountain, broken as the way had been, there had been life. I had seen fresh tracks of animals, and we had noted birds, even though their number had been few. But here were no such signs of life. We were down from the bare rock and into the first circle of vegetation to find that this had a strange look. The green of the narrow bush leaves was lighter in shade than that we had always known, and the very shape of the leaves had a shriveled appearance as if they had been born from blighted seeds.

It was when we came out at the head of a valley that I called a halt. The territory below was even more unbelievable than that we had sighted from the pass. At first I could not really tell the nature of what I looked upon. Then, glancing about me, the sight of seedlings spreading from that growth gave me the answer to that choked gap. They must be trees, for no bush grew to such a height, but they were no normal tree. And they must have grown so for centuries of time, for they completely filled the valley, their tips reaching only a few feet below the rocky point on which we now stood.

Sometime in the distant past they had begun as might any normal tree, but when their boles had reached perhaps ten feet above the ground surface they had taken a sharp bend left or right. After proceeding in that new direction for some feet, they again pointed skyward, to repeat the process again and again, lacing a vast criss-cross of such branched levels, with the true ground of the valley

far below. To cross this we would have to walk the branches, for the woven growth gave no chance of penetration
any lower, which meant balancing from limb to limb, with
fear that a slip meant either a bone breaking fall or even
impalement on one of those shooting uptips.

I edged back from our vantage point. "For this I want
a full day."

Kaththea shaded her eyes from the last sun rays, reflected glitteringly from some quartz in the rocks. "That is truth.
But it is cold here—where can we shelter?"

Kemoc found protection, a crevice about which we piled
other stones until the three of us, huddling closely into
that crack, could endure the chill. There was wood, but
none of us suggested a fire. Who knew what eyes might
pick up a spark on a mountain side where no spark should
rightly be, or what might be drawn to investigate such
a phenomena? Kemoc and I had lain rough before, and
Kaththea made no complaint, we putting her between us
and bringing the blankets about us all.

If the mountain had seemed dead, a lifeless world in
daytime, that was not true at night. There was the wail
of a snow cat that had missed its kill, and a hooting from
the air over the choked valley.

But nothing came near us as we dozed, awoke to listen, and then slept again through a night which also was
different this side of the mountain—one far too long.

VII

In the early morning we ate the last crumbs of journey
bread, and discovered there were only a few sips of water
left in the saddle bottles we had filled at the streamside.
Kemoc shook his bag over his hand.

"It would seem we now have another very good reason to push on," he remarked.

I ran my tongue over my lip and tried to think back to the last really filling meal I had eaten. That was hard doing, for I had lived more or less on emergency rations since Kemoc's summons had taken me from camp. We had seen no trace of game—yet a snow cat had yowled in the night and one of those hunters would not be prowling a preyless land. I visualized a prong-buck steak or even a grass burrower, sizzling on a spit over a fire. And that provided me impetus to approach the verge and survey the springy bough road we must travel.

We made what precautions we could, using the rope once again to unite us, so that a slip need not be fatal. But it was not with any great confidence that any of us faced that crossing. We could not aim straight for the other rim, but had to angle down the length of the branch filled cut in order to keep moving east to the presumed lowlands. The mist still clung there and we could only hope that there *were* lowlands to be found.

I had always held that I had a good head for heights, but in my mountaineering I had trod on solid stone and earth, not on a footing which swayed and dipped, giving to my weight with every step. And I was only a few feet out on that surface when I discovered, almost to my undoing, that this weird valley had inhabitants.

There was a sharp chattering cry; and from the upthrust branch tip, to which I had just reached a hand for a supporting grip, burst a thing which swooped on skin wings and skittered ahead to disappear again into the masking foliage.

Kaththea gave a startled cry and I found my hold on the branch very necessary, for I was almost unbalanced by my start. So our advance became even more slow.

Three times more we sent flitters flying from our path. Once we needed to make an exhausting detour when we sighted another and more frightening inhabitant of this tree top maze, a scaled thing which watched us unblinkingly, a narrow forked tongue flickering from its green lips —for it was colored much like the silver-green of the leaves among which it lay. It was not a serpent, for it had small limbs and clawed feet with which to cling, yet it was e-longated of body, and its whole appearance was malefic. Nor did it fear us in the least.

All time has an end. Sweating, weary from tension to the point of swimming heads and shaking bodies, we made the last step from the quivering boughs to the solid rock of the valley rim. Kaththea dropped to the ground, panting. All of us bore raw scratches and the red marks left by lashing branches. While our field uniforms were sturdy enough to withstand hard usage, Kaththea's robe was torn in many places, and there were bits of broken twig snarled in hair ends which had escaped from the kerchief into which she had knotted them before beginning that journey.

"I would seem to be one of the Moss Ones," she commented with a small, slightly uncertain smile.

I looked back at the way we had come. "This is proper country for such," I said idly. Then silence drew my attention back to my companions. Both of them were staring at me with an intensity which had no connection with what I had just said, or so I thought, but as if I had uttered some profound fact.

"Moss Ones," Kaththea repeated.

"The Krogan, the Thas, the People of Green Silences, the Flannan," Kemoc added.

"But those are legend—tales to amuse children, to frighten the naughty, or to amuse," I protested.

"They are those who are foreign to Estcarp," Kaththea pointed out. "What of Volt? He, too, was dismissed as legend until Koris and our father found his Hole and him waiting. And did not Koris bring forth from there that great axe which was only legend too? And the sea serpent of Sulcar song—not even the most learned ever said that that was only fantasy."

"But women of moss who seek a human mother to nurse

71

their children and who pay in pale gold and good fortune, beings who fly on wings and torment those who strive to learn their secrets, creatures who dwell blindly underground and are to be feared lest they draw a man after them into eternal darkness, and people akin to trees with powers over all growth . . ." I recalled scraps and bits of those tales, told to amuse with laughter, or bring delightful shivers up the back of those who listened to terror while sitting snug and secure by a winter fire in a strongly held manor.

"Those stories are as old as Estcarp," Kemoc said, "and perhaps they reach beyond Estcarp . . . to some other place."

"We have enough to face without evoking phantoms," I snapped. "Do not put one behind each bush for us now."

Yet one could not stifle the working of imagination and this was the type of land which could give rise to such legends. Always, too, there was the reality of Volt which my father had helped to prove. And, as we advanced, my mind kept returning to shift old memories for descriptions of those fantastic beings in the stories.

We were definitely on a down slope, though the broken character of the land continued. Now our greatest need was for water. Though the vegetation grew heavily hereabouts, we came across no stream nor spring, and the growing heat of the day added to our discomfort. The mist still clung, and thus at times we could see only a short distance ahead. And that mist had a steamy quality, making us long to throw aside our helms and mail which weighed so heavy.

I do not know just when I became aware that we were not alone in that steam wreathed wilderness. Perhaps fatigue and the need for water had dulled my scouting sense. But it grew on me that we were under observation. And so sure was I of that, that I waved my companions to cover in the thickets and drew my dart gun as I studied the half concealed landscape.

"It is there . . . somewhere." Kemoc had his weapon in hand also.

Kaththea sat with closed eys, her lips parted a little, her whole attitude one of listening, perhaps not with the ears, but with a deeper sense.

"I cannot touch it," she said in a whisper. "There is no contact—"

"Now it is gone!" I was as sure of that as if I had seen the lurker flitting away as the skinned flapped things had done in the tree valley. I beckoned them on, having now only the desire to put distance between us and whatever had skulked in our wake.

As we moved into yet lower land the mist disappeared. Here the trees and high brush gave way to wide, open glades. Many of these were carpeted by thick, springy growth of gray moss. And I had a faint distate for walking on it, though it cushioned the step and made the going more comfortable.

Bird calls sounded, and we saw small creatures in the moss lands. There was a chance for hunting now, but water remained our major desire. Then we came upon our first trace of man—a crumbling wall, more than half buried or tumbled from its estate as boundary for a field. The growth it guarded was tall grass, but here and there showed the yellow-ripe head of a grain stalk, wizened and small, reverting to the wild grass from which it had evolved. Once this had been a farm.

We took one side of that wall for a guide and so came into the open. The heat of the sun added to our distress, but a farm meant water somewhere near. Kaththea stumbled and caught at the wall.

"I am sorry," her voice was low and strained. "I do not think I can go much farther."

She was right. Yet to separate in this place of danger

• • •

Kemoc supported her. "Over there." He pointed to where a stand of trees grew to offer a patch of shade. When we reached those we discovered another piece of good fortune, for there was a fruit laden vine on the wall. The red globes it bore I recognized as a species of grape, tart and mouth-puckering even when ripe as these were, but to be welcomed now for the moisture they held. Kemoc began to pick all within reach, passing his harvest to Kaththea.

"There is water somewhere, and we must have it." I dropped my pack, checked again the loading of my dart gun, then slung the straps of two of the saddle bottles over my shoulder.

"Kyllan!" Kaththea swallowed a mouthful of pulp hurriedly. "Keep in mind touch!"

But Kemoc shook his head. "I think not—unless you need us. There is no need to arouse anything."

So he felt it too, the sensation that we did not walk through an empty world, that there was here that which was aware of us, waiting, measuring, studying. . . .

"I will think of water, and water only." I do not know just why that assertion seemed important. But I did walk away from them concentrating on a spring, a stream, building up in my mind a vivid mental picture of what I sought.

The walled field was separated from another of its kind; perhaps the gap between them marked some roadway long since overgrown. I caught sight, in the second enclosure, of a prong-horn family group at graze. The buck was larger than any of his species I had known in Estcarp, standing some four feet at the shoulder, his horns a ruddy pair of intricate spirals in the sunlight. He had three does, their lesser horns glistening black, lacking the ringing of the male's. And there were four fawns and an almost grown yearling. The latter was my prize.

Darts are noiseless save for the faint hiss of their ejection. The yearling gave a convulsive leap and fell. For a second or two its companions lifted their heads to regard the fallen with round-eyed stares. Then they took fright and headed in great bounds for the far end of the ancient field, while I leaped the wall and went to my kill.

It was while I was butchering that the sound of water reached my ears, the steady, rippling gurgle of what could only be a swiftly flowing stream. Having made a bundle of meat inside the green hide, I shouldered the package and followed that sound.

Not a stream, but a river, was what I slid down a high bank to find. There was a good current, and a scattering of large rocks around which the water washed with some force.

I ran forward and knelt to drink from my cupped hands. The flood was mountain born, for it was cold, and it was good to fill my mouth and then splash it over my bared head, upon my sweating face. For a long moment or two I was content merely to revel in the touch of water, the wonderful taste of water. Then I rinsed out the saddle bottles, filled each to the brim and hammered in their stoppers, making certain not to lose a drop.

Food and drink—and Kaththea and Kemoc waiting for both. With the heavy bottles dragging at my side, and the prong-horn meat on my shoulder, I started to retrace my trail. but to climb the bank at this point, so burdened, would not be easy. I needed two hands—thus I moved to the right, seeking a gap in the earth barrier.

What I came upon in rounding a stream curve was another reminder that this land had once been peopled. But this was no ruins of a house, nor any building I could recognize. There was a platform of massive blocks, now overgrown in parts with grass and moss. And rising from that sturdy base was a series of pillars—not set in aisles, but in concentric circles. I doubted, after surveying them, whether they had ever supported any roofing. And the reason for such an erection was baffling. It was plain curiosity which betrayed me, for I stepped from raw earth onto the platform, and walked between two of the nearest pillars.

Then . . . I was marching at a slow, set pace around the circle, and I could not break free. Round and round, spiraling ever to the middle of the maze. From that core came forth—not a greeting—but a kind of gloating recognition that prey was advancing to its maw, a lapping tongue from which my whole nature revolted. A complete

75

and loathsome evil, as if I had been licked by a black foulness whose traces still befouled my shrinking skin.

The attack was so utterly racking that I think I cried out, shaken past the point of courage. And if I screamed with throat and tongue, so did I scream with mind, reaching for any help which might exist, in a blindly terrified call for aid.

That came—I was not alone. Strength flowed in, made union with me, tightened to hold against the licking of what dwelt in this stone web. There was another contact and that touch snapped. Satisfaction and desire became anger. I set my hand to a pillar, pulled myself backward, broke the pattern of my steady march.

Pillar hold by pillar hold I retreated, and in me held that defense against the raging entity I could not see. Rage fed upon frustration and bafflement. And then the confidence began to fray. The thing that lurked here had been bloated with constant success; it had not met any counter to its power. And that fact that it could not sweep me in easily for its feeding now worried it.

I had clawed my way to the outer row of the pillar circle when it launched one last attack. Black—I could see the wave of black foulness flowing towards me. I think I cried out again, as I threw myself on with a last surge of energy. My foot caught, and I was falling—into the dark, the black, the very opposite of all that life meant to me.

I was vilely ill—of that I was conscious first, as if there were some substance in my body now being violently rejected by my flesh. And I was retching miserably as I opened my eyes, to find Kemoc supporting me through those wrenching spasms. For the time, only my illness was real. Then, as my brother lowered me to the ground, I levered myself up, to stare wildly about, fearful that I still lay within the pillar way.

But around me was open field, clean and wide under a late afternoon sun which held no hint of any threatening shadows. As Kaththea leaned over me to hold one of the

76

water bottles to my lips I tried to raise my hand to her and found that gesture was beyond my power.

Her face had a strange, closed look; her mouth was set. Beyond her Kemoc was on one knee, his eyes roving, as if he feared attack.

"Evil—" Kaththea cradled my heavy head on her arm. "But thank the Power it was tied to its own sink hole! There is indeed peril in this land. The stench of it hangs to warn us. . . ."

"How did I get here?" I whispered.

"When it took you—or strove to take you—you summoned. And we came. When you reeled out of that trap we brought you away, lest it have greater range than its own cold web—but it did not." She raised her head, looked from side to side; her nostrils expanded as she drew in deep breaths of the warm air. "This is sweet and clean, and wishes hurt to nothing—empty of all threat. Yet there you stumbled on a pocket of evil, very ancient evil, and where there is one we are likely to find another."

"What kind of evil?" I asked. "Kolder—?" Even as I gave the name of that old arch enemy, I was sure it did not answer what I had stumbled upon by the river.

"I never knew Kolder, but I do not think this is of that ilk. This is evil, as of . . . the Power!" She gazed down at me as if she herself could not believe in what she said.

Kemoc broke in sharply: "That is a contradiction which cannot stand!"

"So would I have said before today. Yet, I tell you, this was born not from any alien force, but in a twisted way from what we have known all our lives. Can I not recognize my learning, my weapons, even when distorted and debased? Distorted and debased is this thing, and for that reason perhaps the greater menace to us, as it carries in it a minute particle of the familiar. What happened here to turn all we know utterly vile?"

But there was no reply for her. She rested the palm of her hand flat against my forehead, and stooped far over me so that her eyes looked directly into mine. Again from

77

her lips came a low chant, and her actions drew out of me, mind and body, the rest of the wrenching nausea and terrible revulsion, leaving only the warning memory of what had happened and must never happen so again.

A measure of my energy restored, we went on. The open field had been security of a kind, but with night so close upon us we wanted shelter. Thus we followed the walls until we came to a small rise with on it a mound of stones, some of which still held together in an angle of what once might have been the corner of a building.

Together Kemoc and I worked to loosen more and build up a barricade before that triangular space while Kaththea roamed about the rise gathering sticks, and now and then breaking off a bit of growing thing. When she returned she was lighter of countenance.

"There is no rank smell here—rather, once there must have dwelt nearby one who followed the healing arts. Herbs will grow without tending, once they are well rooted. And look what I have found." She spread out her harvest on top of a squared block of stone.

"This"—one finger touched a slip of what could be fern —"is saxfage, which gives sweet sleep to the fevered. And this"—a stem with four trifid leaves— "langlorn, which brightens the mind and clears the senses. Best of all, which may be the reason that the other fair herbs have continued to grow—Illbane—Spirit Flower."

That I knew of, since it was the old, old custom even in Estcarp to plant such about a doorway in spring, harvest its white flowers in the fall and dry them, to wreath above the main entrance to any house and stable. Such action brought good luck, prevented the entrance of ill fortune, and also had an older meaning—that any power of evil be baffled by its scent. For it was the nature of the plant that, picked or broken, its aromatic odor lingered for a long time.

Kaththea built a fire, laying her pieces with the care of one constructing a work of significance. When I would have protested such revealment of our presence, Kemoc

78

shook his head, laying fingertip to lips in warning. Then, when she had her sticks laid, she crushed between her palms the saxfage and langlorn, working the mass into the midst of the wood. Last of all she carefully broke two blossoms from her spray of Illbane and added those also. Taking up the stem with its remaining tip cluster of flowers, she began to walk back and forth along our small barricade, brushing the stones we had set there with it, then planting the bruised spray among the rocks as a small banner.

"Light the fire," she bade us. "It will not betray; rather, it will guard this night. For nothing which is truly of the dark will find in it, smoke and flame, that which it can face."

So I set spark and the flames arose. The smoke was spiced with the smell of herbs. And shortly thereafter came another fine aroma as we toasted fresh meat on spits of wood. Perhaps Kaththea had indeed wrought strong magic, for I no longer felt that eyes saw, ears listened, that we were overwatched in this strange land.

VIII

WE SLEPT well that night, too deep for the troubling of dreams, to awake rested and clear-eyed, with only memory's warning against what must walk here. But Kaththea must have awakened the first, for when I roused she knelt, her crossed arms on our barrier, gazing out into the morning land. There was no sun, only clouds prolonging the half-light of the early hours into the day.

She turned her head as I stirred. "Kyllan, what do you make of that?"

My gaze followed her pointing finger. There was a copse of trees some distance away and from beyond that a glow reached the sky. Not the red of fire flame, but a greenish radiance, which clearly was from no natural cause.

"It remains always the same, neither waning nor waxing."

"A beacon of sorts?" I hazarded.

"Perhaps. But to summon—or to guide—what? I do not remember that we saw it last night. But I have listened and there is naught to hear."

I knew that she had not listened with her ears, but with her seer-trained inner sense.

"Kaththea—"

She turned her head to look at me.

"This land may be full of such traps as I blundered into. There may be good reason why it was closed and is closed to those of our mother's blood."

"All that is true. Yet it has come to me that there was a purpose beyond our own wills guiding us here, Kyllan. Save for such plague spots as you found, this is a fair land. Look about you. Even under the shadow of the clouds, do you not find it in you to have a liking for these fields?"

She was right. There was an odd drawing in me, a desire to walk those ancient, overgrown fields, even to thrust my hands deep into their waiting soil. I wanted to fling off the heaviness of helm and mail, to run joyously free and unburdened, with the wind about me and a fresh land under my feet. I had not felt so since I had been a small boy already under the hammer of Otkell's discipline.

Kaththea nodded. "You see? Can you turn your back on all this merely because it suffers from some disease? We can beware of the places of evil, and make the best of those of good. I tell you such herbs as I harvested last night cannot grow where all is befouled by the Powers of the Dark."

"No matter how fair a land," Kemoc said from behind

us, "a man must have two things—a shelter and a supply of food. I do not believe this is what we want for a home roof-tree or hall. And for awhile we must turn hunters for food. Also, I would like to know a little more of our neighbors."

With that I agreed. It is always best to be sure that any shadow pooled behind a tree is only shadow and not sheltering some unpleasant surprise.

We ate more of the meat and drank the tart vine fruit, and then we prepared to journey on. Though before Kaththea left the hill she again plucked a selection of herbs, bagging them in a strip torn from the hem of her robe, which she now proceeded to shorten to only slightly below knee length.

The gleam, still faintly visible because of the clouds, drew us. But we went warily, taking to the cover of the woods. Kaththea reported no troublesome scents and the small copse seemed normal with birds and other wild life. This woods was not too wide and finally we reached a fringe of brush on its far side. Here again was open country and through it wound the river. In a curve of that stream stood the first real structure we had seen this side of the mountains. And it was familiar in shape—one of the watchtower-guard-keeps such as we had been housed in many times in Estcarp. From the slit windows of the third and fourth levels issued the light, and more was difused from the crown, where were the only evidences of age, a few stones missing from parapet gaps.

Looking upon it I had not the slightest desire to explore further. It had not met us with an active slap of evil such as I had met in the stone web . . . but there was an eerie sense of withdrawal, a signpost without words to ward off the coming of men. Whatever walked there might not be actively antagonistic to our species, but neither would we be welcomed by it. As to how I knew this, I cannot explain. But Kemoc agreed with me.

Kaththea centered upon it her "seeing," then shook her head. "There is no penetration of mind, and I would not try in body. Let be what lies there, if anything does. There are and have always been forces which are not actively good or evil—they can kill or cure. But to meddle with them is risky; it is best not to awaken them."

Still I had a distaste for being observed by anything or anyone manning that post. The others agreed to slip back into the wood and circle under its cover to the river. We kept downstream from the site of the pillar web, Kaththea sniffing the wind for any warning of ill.

Though it did not rain, yet the gloom of the clouds continued as we followed the stream for a guide. And this country was more wooded and therefore dark. Then I sighted the fresh tracks of one of the large, flightless birds which are esteemed excellent eating in Estcarp. They being most wary, I thought it best to hunt alone, promising faithfully that I would not fall under any enticement because of curiosity. I stripped off pack and water bottle, and even my helm, lest its chain mail throat scarf give forth some small clink of noise.

It was plain that the birds fed in beds of riverside wild grain, but tall reeds arose nearby, promising cover. However, I was not to reach my quarry. Warning came in a movement across the stream.

Drift from past high water had gathered on a sand bank there, piling up a causeway. In and among that tangle were slinking shadows—black, agile, so swift of movement that I could not truly make out what manner of creature they were. Yet the very stealth of their approach, the concentration of their numbers, was a warning. As if they knew or sensed my uneasiness, they came the faster, more and more of them. The first plunged into the water, its narrow snout cutting a V across the current.

Only the swiftness of the current delayed their determination, carrying them well downstream. Yet I was certain they would make a landing there somewhere. And they were not hunting the birds, but me!

Trouble—head for the open—the nearest field.

As I thought that alarm I got to my feet and ran for the

open. The slinking advance of these things needed cover; in the open they could be met more effectively.

Kemoc acknowledged and signalled me to the right. Now I slowed my retreat, walking backwards, having no wish to be rushed from behind. And my precautions proved to be well taken when the first of that black pack darted from a bush to the massive roots of a fallen tree in my sight a few moments later.

I was moving through shoulder high bush, and this was unpleasant country through which to be so stalked. There were too many excellent sites for ambush. Animals! Perhaps I had been too shocked from my experience with the web thing. I had been able to control animals before, so there was no reason why I might not again. I sent an exploring thought to what lurked behind the tree roots.

No animal—no normal animal! What? A red madness of kill, kill, tear and devour—an insanity which was not animal, but raw fury combined with cunning on another level. There was no control for this, only revulsion and the fear that the sane can feel for the chaotic depths of complete unbalance! Again I had erred, for my contact aroused them even more, flamed their hunger to a higher pitch. Also there were many—too many—

I wanted to run, to burst through the brush which was now a prison restraining me to be pulled down and slain at their pleasure. But I forced myself to move slowly, dart gun ready, watching for any slinker that came within range.

The bushes became smaller . . . then I was free, out in a wide stretch of open. Some distance away Kemoc and Kaththea moved, heading for the very center of that space. But with the pack coming . . . How could we stand them all off?

In my eagerness to reach the others I stumbled and went down. I heard Kaththea cry out, and flung myself over, to see the black creatures flow eagerly toward me. They ran silently, not as hounds that give tongue in the hunt, and that silence added to their uncanniness.

83

They were short of leg, though that did not impair their speed, and their bodies were sleekly furred, very lithe and agile. Their heads were narrow, pointing sharply to muzzles where yellow fangs showed against their dark hides. Their eyes were small specks of red fire.

Since I dared not take time to get to my feet I fired as I lay. The leader of that pack curled up, biting savagely at a dart in its shoulder. Yet even in pain and rage the thing made no outcry. However, the mishap of their leader gave the rest of the pack pause. They scattered back into cover, leaving the writhing wounded one behind until its struggles were stilled.

I ran for where Kaththea and Kemoc stood.

Kemoc was waiting with ready gun. "Hunters," he said. "Where did they come from?"

"They crossed the river," I panted. "I have never seen their kind before—"

"Haven't you?" Kaththea held her bundle of herbs pressed tight against her breast as if in those withering bits of twig, leaf and stem she had a shield to withstand all danger. "They are rasti."

"Rasti?" How could one associate a rodent perhaps as long as a mid-finger with these three-foot, insane hunters? Yet, when I considered the appearance of the creatures, apart from their size, I could see the resemblance. Perhaps not true rasti, but of the same family, grown to gigantic proportions for their species and with even worse ferocity than their midget brethren displayed. To so identify them removed some of the fear of the unknown that had been part of their impact upon me.

"And rasti are not so easily turned from any prey," Kemoc pointed out. "Have you never seen them drag down a fowl in a well-protected farmyard?"

I had once, and that memory made me flinch. Circling —yes, they were beginning to circle us now, as they had that doomed fowl on that long past day. More and more of them squirmed out of the wood, bellies flat to earth as if they were snakes rather than warm-blooded furred things.

THREE AGAINST THE WITCH WORLD

No need to warn Kemoc—he was firing. Three black things leaped in the air, beat at and clawed the ground. But a gun can continue to fire only as long as it is loaded. How long could our limited supply of darts last? We had our swords, but to wait until rasti came into range for cutting work was to open our defense to only one probable end.

"I cannot—the Power will not work against them!" Kaththea's voice was shrill. "They have nothing I can reach!"

"These will reach them!" I fired again, striving to pick the best shot possible. But it seemed that nature was ranged against us now in more than one fashion. For the darkness of the clouds approached night and suddenly a downpour of rain burst upon us, with force enough to buffet our bodies. However, it did not make our enemy retreat.

"Wait—look there!"

I missed my shot at Kemoc's cry and snarled at him as a snow cat might after an aborted hunting leap. Then I saw what was coming. A horse—at least in this gloom it seemed to be a horse—pounded on at a gallop. And on it was a rider. The figure came up between us and the rasti pack. Then my eyes were dazzled by a burst of white, searing light. It seemed that that rider called down lightning to serve as a lash with which to beat the earth about the skulking hunters.

Three times that lash fell, blinding us. Then I caught a dim sight of mount and rider galloping on, lost in the wood once again, while from the earth where that strange weapon had smote arose smoking trails of vapor. Nothing else moved.

Without a word Kemoc and I caught Kaththea between us and ran—away from that place, out of the open and the pouring rain. We gained the shelter of a tree and crouched together as if we were all one.

I heard Kaththea speak close to my ear. "That—that was of the Power—and for good, not ill. But it did not answer me!" Her bewilderment held a note of hurt. "Listen"—her fingers gripped both of us— "I have remembered something. Running water—if we can find a place in the midst of running water, and bless it, then we are safe."

"Those rasti swam the river," I protested.

"True. But we were not in the midst of running water on a blessed place. We must find such."

I had no wish to return to the river; as far as I could see most of the evil we had met with so far had been connected with that stretch of water. It would be better to try and follow the rider—

"Come!" Kaththea urged us out into the fury of the storm. "I tell you, this dark, together with wind and water, may release other things—we must find a safe place."

I was unconvinced, but I also knew that no argument of mine would make any impression on her. And Kemoc advanced no protest. We went on, the rain beating us, as that rider had lashed the ground which now showed great slashes of seared black vegetation and earth. At least I was able to convince Kaththea to head in the direction where the rider had disappeared.

Here the wooded land was less densely grown. I thought we had stumbled on some track or road, for we found the footing easier. And that track did bring us to the river. Kaththea could have claimed foresight, for there, in the midst of the rain-pitted and rising river, was an islet of rock. Drift had caught at one end, and a point in the center made a natural watchtower.

"We had better get over before the water is any higher," Kemoc said.

Whether we might or not, burdened with packs and weapons, I was not sure. Kaththea broke from us, was already wading through the shallows. She was waist deep and battling the pull of the current before we reached her. The fact that we entered the stream above the narrow tip of the island was in our favor, as the current bore us down upon it and we crawled out on the tip very little wetter than the rain had already left us.

Nature had fashioned an easily-defended keep, with a rock walled space for a hall and the watch point above.

A short survey proved we had come ashore on the only place possible for a landing. Elsewhere the rocks gave no foothold, but reared up small cliffs from the water's foaming edge. Should the rasti come after us, we would have only a narrow strip to defend, so they could not possibly draw their fatal ring.

"This is a free place, not touched by any ill," Kaththea told us. "Now I shall seal it so." From her packet of herbs she brought out a stalk of Illbane, crushing it tightly in her fist, then holding her hand to her lips while she alternately breathed upon and chanted over what she held. At length she went forward on hands and knees, scrubbing the mass of vegetation into the rocky way up which we had come from the water. Then she was back with us, leaning against a stone, limp as one spent after hours of hard labor.

The violence of the rain did not long continue, though the river water continued to boil about our refuge. Storm gusts receded into a drizzle, which at length pattered into silence.

Speculation concerning the rider who had saved us continued to exercise most of my thought. Kaththea had declared the stranger to be one who used the Power rightly, if not in her way. That other had not replied to my sister's attempt for communication, but that did not mean enmity. The fact that such service had been rendered spoke of good will. Thus far we had come across no other sign of any natives. Unless one could count the horror of the web, and that which *might* have garrisoned the watch-keep as inhabitants.

My glimpse of the rider had been so limited by the gloom and the storm that I was sure only that he had a reasonably human shape, that he was a horseman of no mean ability, and that he had known exactly how to put rasti to route. Beyond that was ignorance.

But the thought of horses in this land also gave me material to chew upon. Since I had bestrode my first pony when I had had no more than four summers behind me,

I have never willingly gone afoot. After we had left the Torgians on the other side of the range a kind of loss had plagued me. Now—if there were mounts to be had in this land the sooner we obtained them the better! Mounted, we need not have feared the rasti.

Tomorrow we must hunt in our turn, trace that galloping rescuer, and learn what manner of men shared this wilderness. . . .

Look! Be quiet—

Two orders, one beamed over the other in Kemoc's haste.

Out over the surface of the turbulent stream a bird wheeled, dipped and soared. There was a shimmer to its wings, a glint which I had never seen reflected from feathers before, as it approached our refuge.

Food. . . .

Kemoc's suggestion made me aware of hunger. We did not lack water this time, but we did food—our packet of prong-horn meat having been lost in the rasti hunt. Unless we could hook some stream dweller out of the flood, we would fast this night. The bird was large enough to provide a scanty meal. But to shoot it unless directly overhead would send it down to be swept away by the current.

My brother drew his gun, then Kaththea's hand shot forward, slapping down his.

"No!" she cried aloud.

Closer the bird swung; then, after a downward plunge, it settled on the rocks of our refuge and began to sidle around that rough way in our direction.

The shimmering quality of its plumage was even more pronounced at close range, white and pure, yet overlaid with radiant sheen. Bill and feet were a clear, bright red, the eyes dark and large. It halted and folded its wings, sat watching us as if awaiting some meaningful move on our part. All idea of feeding on the creature faded rapidly from my mind.

Kaththea studied it as intently as the bird appeared to

be observing us. Then, lifting her right hand, our sister tossed a small crumpled leaf at the winged visitor. The long neck twisted and the head darted forward; bright eyes inspected her offering.

The shimmering became even brighter. My sister uttered some words in a tone of command, brought her hands together with a sharp clap. There was a shimmer of mist, then it cleared before us. The bird was gone—what teetered on a rock perch was still winged but no bird.

IX

"FLANNAN!" I whispered, unable to believe that my eyes were not bedazzled by some sorcery.

The creature might not be the ethereal thing legend has reported in tales, but it was not a bird and it did have characteristics which were akin—outwardly—to the human.

The feet were still clawed and red, yet they were not the stick-proportions of a true bird; the body had taken on a humanoid shape with arms showing beneath the half spread wings, and tiny hands at the end of those arms. The neck might still be long and supple, but the head it supported, though centered by a jutting beak, held a recognizable face. The white shimmering feathers clothed it, save for feet, arms and hands.

It was blinking rapidly and those tiny hands lifted in a gesture toward Kaththea as if warding off some blow it feared.

Flannan, the air-borne race. . . . My memory presented

gleanings from half a hundred old stories, and I thought
fleetingly that perhaps it was well for us now that we had
all had a liking in childhood for listening to old legends.
The Flannan were friendly to man after a somewhat skit-
tish fashion, for they quickly lost interest in any project,
had small powers of concentration, and were very apt to
leave any undertaking far from finished. The heroes and
heroines of many stories had come to grief by depending
upon a Flannan past its desire to render aid. However,
never had it made any alliance with dark forces.

Kaththea began a crooning sing-song, close to a bird's
trill. The Flannan sidled a little closer, its long neck twist-
ing. Then its beak opened and it trilled back. My sister
frowned, was silent a moment before she replied—to be
interrupted by a trill in higher note. A pause, then it sang
longer, and this time I was sure that sound held the rasp
of impatience.

"It responds," Kaththea told us, "to the invocation of
shared power, but I cannot read its answer. And I do not
believe that it practices shape changing of its own accord."

"Sent to spy on us?" Kemoc wondered.

"Perhaps."

"Then it could guide us to the one who sent it!" I was
still thinking of the rider.

Kaththea laughed. "Only if it wishes, unless you can
grow wings and take to the air in its wake."

She brought out her packet of herbs and picked free
Illbane. On the palm of her hand she held it towards the
Flannan. The creature looked from the withered herb to
Kaththea, plainly in question. A little of my sister's frown
lightened.

"At least legend holds true so far. This is not the messenger of any ill force. So—" Once again she broke into
song, this time slowly, with space between notes.

The Flannan cocked its head in a bird-like pose. When
it trilled in reply, its answer, too, was slower, so that I
was able to detect individual notes. Once or twice Kaththea nodded as if she had caught one she could translate.

"It was sent to watch us. This is a land where evil interlocks with good, and the pools of evil may overflow from time to time. Its message is for us to retreat, to return whence we came."

"Who sent it?" My demand was blunt.

Kaththea trilled. The Flannan's long neck curved, it looked to me, and I could read nothing, not even interest, in that regard. It made no answer. Kaththea repeated her query, this time sharply. When it remained silent, she traced a symbol by finger tip in the air between them.

The reaction to this was startling. There was a squawk, and the half-human aspect of the Flannan vanished. We saw a bird once more. It spread wings and took off, flying three times counterclockwise about the islet, while each time it passed us it shrieked. My sister's eyes were ablaze and her hands moved in a series of sharp gestures as she chanted some words in the seer tongue. The bird faltered and squawked again, then flew straight as a dart's flight north.

"So—well, that will not work!" Kaththea broke out. "I may not be a sworn witch, but I have more Power than a thrice-circle set by such as *that* can confine!"

"What was it trying to do?" I asked.

"A piece of very elementary magic." My sister made a sound close to a snort of contempt. "It was laying a thrice-circle to keep us pinned on this spot. If that is the best the one who sent it can do, then we can beat it on all points."

"When it went north, could it have been returning to the one who sent it?" Kemoc put my own question aloud.

"I think so. It is the nature of the Flannan not to be able to hold any purpose long in mind. And the fact that I defeated it could send it back to the source in panic."

"Then north lies what we seek."

"Northward went the rider also," I added.

"And north would take us once more past the web, and the silent keep, and perhaps other pitfalls. There must come a time when we have clear sight . . ." There was an odd note of hesitation in her voice, drawing our attention to her.

Kaththea stared down at her hands, as I had seen her sit before, cupping in their apparent emptiness something in which she could read the future, and it would seem that was not a bright one.

"To be only half of a thing is never easy," she continued. "This we have always known. I did not take the oath and I have never worn the Jewel of the sisterhood. Yet, save for those two things, I am a witch. There is one other step I did not take, which was forbidden to one not sworn and bound by seer oaths. Yet now this might serve, even save us."

"No!" Kemoc knew, though I did not, what she hinted. His hands went to cup her chin, bringing up her head so that he might look straight into her eyes. "No!" he repeated, with such force that his cry might have been a battle shout.

"So we continue to walk into hidden peril, when by so much we may be able to guard, and guide?" she asked.

"And you would do this thing, knowing all the danger which lies in it? We have no time for rank folly either, Kaththea. Think—how many even of the sisterhood have taken this grave step? And when it is done they must have the aid of the Power to the highest degree. And—"

"And, and, and!" she interrupted him. "Do not believe all you have heard, Kemoc. It is the nature of any organization of Wise Ones that they make mysteries to awe those who have not their gifts. Yes, it is true that few Witches now have this aid, but in Estcarp there was little reason for it. What need had they to explore? They knew their country intimately, both as it was and as it had been for countless years. They have not ventured for centuries into territory so strange they must have a delegate. It was our father and mother, not the Witches, who went up against the Kolder. And in their time the Kolder sealed off Gorm. But here is no alien force, only that which we know in part.

Though it may be warped or changed in some particulars. Thus no better aid could we summon—"

"What does she mean?" I appealed to Kemoc.

"A Familiar's birth," he replied. His face was as set as it had been on that ride to bring Kaththea forth from the Place.

"A Familiar?" I did not yet know what he meant. What was a Familiar?

Kaththea raised her hands and took Kemoc's wrists so that she could set aside his grasp on her chin. She did not look at me when she answered, but at him as if she would impose her will so that he could not deny her desire.

"I must make a servant, Kyllan. One which will explore not this country as we see it, walk it, sense it, but who can return to the past and witness what chanced here and what can be done in the present for our preservation."

"And how must she do this?" Kemoc burst out hotly. "As a woman gives birth to a child, so must she in a measure create a being, though this will be born of her mind and spirit, not her flesh! It can be a deadly thing!"

"All birth lays a risk on someone." Kaththea's quiet tone was in such contrast to his anger that it carried more emphasis. "And—if you are both willing—I shall have more than myself to call upon. Never before in Estcarp have there been three like us—is that not so? We can be one after a fashion when there is need. What if we now unite so and will with me—will not the risk be so much the lessened? I would not try this alone, that I swear to you in all truth. Only if you will consent freely and willingly to my aid will this be my path."

"And you think that there is a true need for such an act?" I asked.

"It is a choice between walking into a pit as blindly as I crossed the mountains, or going clear-eyed. The seeds of all perils which lurk here were sown in the past, and time has both nourished and mutated them. But should we dig up those seeds and understand the reason for

93

their sowing, then we can also take guard against the fruit they have borne through the years."

"I will not!" Kemoc was vehement.

"Kemoc . . ." She had not loosed her hold on his hands, and now she spread out the scarred and stiff-fingered one, smoothing its ridged flesh. "Did you say 'I will not' when you went into the fight wherein you got this?"

"But that was far different! I was a man, a warrior—it was my strength against that of those I faced—"

"Why count me as less than yourself?" she countered. "Perhaps my battles may not be fought with dart gun and sword blade, but I have been under as severe a discipline these six years as any warrior could ever know. And I have in that time been set against such enemies as perhaps you cannot even conceive. Nor am I saying now in false confidence that I can do this thing alone—I know that is not the truth. I am bidding you to a fight, to stand with me, which is an easier thing than willing you to stand aside and do nothing while watching another take risks."

His set lips did not relax, but he did not protest again, and I knew that she had won. Perhaps I had not fought on his side because I did not know the danger into which she would venture, but my ignorance was also trust in her. At moments such as these she was no young girl; instead she put on such a robe of authority that the matter of years did not mean much and she was our elder.

"When?" Kemoc surrendered with that word.

"What better time than here and now? Though first we must eat and drink. Strength of body means backing for strength of mind and will."

"The drinking is easy, but the eating . . ." Kemoc looked a little brighter, as if he had discovered in this mundane need an argument for abandoning the whole project.

"Kyllan will provide." Again she did not look at me. But I knew what must be done. And this I had never tried before, save when I had approached it with the Torgians.

When one has even a small share of talent or reflection of the Power, one also knows that there are bounds set upon

94

its use. And to willfully break one such for one's own benefit exacts a price in return. Never since the time I had first learned I could control the minds of beasts had I ever used that to facilitate hunting. I had not sent the Torgians away in peril when I had dispatched them from our camp. Several times I had deterred wild things from attacking or trailing men. But to summon a creature to death for my profit, I sensed, was one of the forbidden things.

But now that was just what I must do, for the good Kaththea would accomplish. Silently I took upon myself the full responsibility for my act, lest the backlash of this perversion of the Power fall upon my sister's sorcery. Then I set myself, intently, to seek and draw the food we must have.

Fish and reptiles, as I had long ago learned, had minds so apart from human kind that they could not be compelled to action—though, in the case of some reptiles, a withdrawing could be urged. But a mammal could be so brought to us. Prong-horns could swim. . . .Mentally I built up as vivid a picture of a prong-horn as memory and imagination combined could create. Holding such a picture then, I cast out my thin line, seeking contact. Never before had I tried to do this thing, for I had dealt with beasts directly under eye, or knew, from other evidence, were nearby. This seeking for no particular animal, but only one of a species, might fail.

But it did not. My spinning thought made contact—and instantly I impressed will, needing to move swiftly to control the animal. Moments later a young prong-horn leaped down the river bank in full sight. I brought it out into the flood at the same angle we had used so that the current would bear it to the islet.

"No!" I forbade Kemoc's use of his gun. The kill was my responsibility in all ways; none of the guilt must go to another. I awaited the animal I had forced to swim to its death, and all I could offer it was a quick, clean end.

Kaththea watched me closely as I dragged up the body. Out of my troubled mind I asked her:

"Will this in any way lessen the Power?"

She shook her head, but there was a shadow in her eyes. "We need only strength of body, Kyllan. But yet . . . you have taken upon yourself a burden. And how great will be your payment, I cannot reckon."

A lessening of my talent, I thought, and put it to mind that I must not trust that in any crisis until I was sure of the extent of my loss. Nor did I take into consideration that this was not Estcarp, that those rules which conditioned witchery in that land might not hold here where the Power had been set adrift into other ways.

We made a fire of drift and ate, forcing ourselves past the first satisfying of hunger, as flames must consume fuel for some necessary degree of heat.

"It is near to night." Kemoc thrust a stick which had spitted meat into the heart of the fire. "Should this not wait upon daybreak? Ours is a force fed by light. Such summoning at the wrong time might bring instead a Power of the dark."

"This is a thing which, begun at sunset, is well begun. If a Familiar be sent forth by the mid-hour of the night, it may rove the farther. Not always are light and dark so opposed, one to the other," Kaththea returned. "Now listen well, for once I have begun this I cannot tell you aught, or explain. We shall clasp hands, and you must join minds as well. Pay no heed to anything my body may do, save do not loose our hand clasp. Above all, no matter what may come, stay with me!"

We needed to make no promises as to that. I feared now for her, as Kemoc did. She was very young for all her seeress training. And, though she seemed very sure of her powers, yet she might also have the overconfidence of the warrior who has not yet been tried in his first ambush.

The clouds which had overhung the day lifted at sunset, and my sister drew us around to face those brilliant flags in the sky, so that we could also see the mountains over which we had come into this haunted land. We joined hands and then minds.

For me it was like that time when our mother had so drawn upon the three of us in her search for our father. There was first the loss of identity, with the knowledge that I must not fight that loss though it went against every instinct of self preservation. After that—a kind of flowing back and forth, in and out . . . a weaving . . . of what?

I do not know how long that period lasted, but I emerged suddenly, my hand jerking wildly. Kaththea was gasping, moaning, her body moved now and again in convulsive shudders. I caught at her shoulder with my free hand, trying to steady her. Then I heard a cry from Kemoc as he came to my aid.

She gave small, sharp ejaculations of pain. And at intervals she writhed so that we could hardly keep the hold we had promised her we would not break. To make it more difficult, I was tired and drained of strength, so that I had to force myself to every movement.

Her eyes were shut. I thought that she must be elsewhere, her body remaining to fight against what she willed it to do. In the light of the now dying fire her face was not only pale, but faintly luminescent, so that we missed no outward sign of her torment.

The end came with a last sharp outcry and arching of her body. From her sprang a dart of—was it flame? Perhaps the size of my hand, it stood upright, sharply brilliant. Then it swayed a little, as might a candle flame in a breeze. Kaththea shuddered again and opened her eyes to look upon what she had brought forth. The flame shape changed, put forth small pinions of light, and became a slender wand between those wings. Kaththea sighed and then said weakly:

"It is not like—"

"Evil?" Kemoc demanded sharply.

"No. But the form is different. That which is here has had a hand in its making. Form does not matter, though. Now—"

With our arms about her in support, she leaned forward to address the winged wand as she had spoken to

97

the Flannan. In our minds we read the meaning of those unknown words. She was repeating ancient formulae, putting this child, or more-than-child, of hers under obedience, setting it to the task it must do.

Back and forth it swayed as she spoke. Her words might have been wind bending it to and fro. The she finished and it stood still and upright. Her last command came dart-swift:

"Go!"

It was gone and we sat in the dark. Kaththea withdrew her hands from ours and pressed them down upon her body as if striving to sooth an ache.

I threw wood on the fire. As the flames climbed, her face showed in their light sunken, old, with a cast of suffering I had seen on men sore wounded. Kemoc cried out and drew her to him, so that her head rested on his shoulder, and his cheeks were wet with more than the sweat called forth by our efforts to feed her energy.

She raised her hand slowly and touched his face. "It is over and we have wrought together very well, my brothers! Our child searches time and space, being bound by neither, and what it learns will serve us well. I do not guess this; I know it. Now, let us sleep. . . ."

Kaththea slept, and Kemoc also. But though I was weary yet still there was a restlessness within me. Fear for Kaththea, no—her travail was over, and anything which could have been perilous for her must already have struck during that struggle. Wariness of attack now? I thought not: we were on safe ground for this night. My own guilt? Perhaps But for that I would not disturb the others. In due time I would pay for what I had done; for the present it would be best to put it out of mind.

I settled down on my blanket, shut my eyes, and strove to invite sleep. Then I started up on one elbow, awake—to listen to a long familiar sound through the night. Not too far away a horse had neighed!

X

I HEARD the sound of hooves pounding turf. And did I or did I not sight the flash of lightning whip on the far shore of the river, that from which the rasti had swum for their attack? But lastly I fixed my mind on the thought of horses and what those might mean to us. In me grew the determination that with the coming of morning light I would go exploring. . . .

As if that decision were an answer to allay my uneasiness, I slept. For the sounds of the hunt, if hunt it could be, died away, while the murmur of the river made a sound to soothe overwrought nerves.

Though I was the last to sleep, I was the first to wake. Our fire had smoldered into dead ash and the dawn was cold, with damp eddying from the water to touch us with moist fingers. I pulled the rest of the bleached wood we had gathered and coaxed a new blaze into life. It was while I knelt so that I saw him—coming down to the water to drink.

Torgians were the finest steeds of Estcarp, but they were not beautiful. Their coats never gleamed, for all the grooming a man could give, nor were they large in frame. But here, raising a dripping muzzle from the water's edge, was such a mount as a man may dream of all his days, yet never see save in those dreams. Big of frame, yet slender of leg, arched of neck, with a black coat which shone like a polished sword blade, a mane and tail rippling as might a maiden's hair—

And once I looked upon that stallion I knew such a longing as I could not stifle. Head raised he faced me across that current. There was no fear in him; curiosity, yes, but no fear. He was of the wild, and I thought he had never had reason to believe that his will could be subordinated to that of any other creature.

For a long moment he stood so, studying me as I moved to the narrow end of the islet. And then, dismissing me as harmless, he drank again, before moving a little into the river, as if he enjoyed the feel of the water about his legs. Looking upon him, his beauty and his proud freedom, I was lost.

Without thought I tried contact, striving to win him so to wait for me, to listen to my desire. Head flung up, he snorted, retreated a step or two for the bank from which he had come. He was curious, yet a little wary. Then I touched what could only be a dim memory—of a rider he had once had . . .

On the shore he waited, watched, as I plunged into the stream, helmless, without the mail or weapons I had laid aside. I swam for the shore and still the stallion stood to watch me, now and then pawing the earth a little impatiently, tossing his head so that the silky mane fluttered out, or flicking his long tail.

He would stand for me! I exulted in my triumph—he was mine! My fears of losing my gift had been foolish; never had my ability to contact an animal mind been so sharp and so quickly successful. With such a horse as this the world was mine! There was only the stallion and me in the early morning—

I waded ashore, unheeding water-soaked garments and the chill of the wind, intent only on the great and wonderful animal waiting for me—for *me!* He lowered his noble head to blow into the palm I held out to him. Then he allowed me to run my hands along his shoulders. He was mine as securely as if I had followed the ancient craft of training wherein a cake of oats and honey carried against my skin for three days and then moistened with my spittle

100

had been given him to eat. Between us there was a bond
of no breaking. That was so clear to me that I had no hesitation in mounting him bareback, and he suffered me to
do so.

He began to trot and I gloried in the strong motion of
his body, the even pacing. In all my years I had never bestrode such force, dignity, beauty, authority. It carried with
it an intoxication greater than any wine a man might sa-
vor. This—this was being a king, a godling out of the
early mists of forgotten time.

Behind us was the river, before us an open world. Just
the two of us, free and alone. A faint questioning rose somewhere deep within me. Two of us?—away from the river?
But there was something back there, something of importance. Under me that mighty body tensed, began to gallop. I twined my fingers deep in the flowing mane which
whipped at my face, and knew a wonderful exultation as
we pounded on across a plain.

There was sunlight now, and still the stallion ran effort-
lessly, as if those muscles could know no fatigue. I believed
he could keep to that flight for hours. But my first exultation paled as the light brightened. The river . . . I glanced
over my shoulder—that dim line far behind marked it.
The river . . . and on it . . .

In my mind there was a click. Kaththea! Kemoc! How,
why had I come to do this? Back—I must head back there.
Without bit or rein I should use my mind to control the
stallion, return him to the river. I set my wish upon him—

No effect. Under me that powerful body still galloped
away from the river, into the unknown. I thrust again, harder now as my faint discomfort became active alarm. Yet
there was no lessening of speed, no turning. Then I strove
to take entire control wholly, as I had with the Torgians
and the prong-horn I had brought to its death.

It was as if I walked across a crust beneath which bubbled a far different substance. If one did not test the
crust it served for a footing, but to strike hard upon it
carried one to what lay below. And in those seconds I

learned the truth. If what I rode carried to my eyes and my surface probing the form of a stallion, it was in reality a very different creature. What it was I could not tell, save that it was wholly alien to all I knew or wished to know.

And also I believed now that I had as much chance of controlling it by my will as I had of containing the full flood of the river in my two hands. I had not mastered a free running horse; I had been taken in as clever a net as had ever been laid for a half bewitched man, for that I must have been from my first sighting of this beast.

Perhaps I could throw myself from its back, though its pace, now certainly swifter than any set by a real horse, could mean injury, even death to follow such a try at escape. Where was it taking me, and for what purpose? I strove frantically to pierce below the horse level of its mind. There was a strong compulsion, yes. I was to be entrapped and then delivered—where and to whom?

Through my own folly this had come upon me. But the peril at the end could be more than mine alone, for what if the other two could then be reached through me? That enchantment which had held from my sighting of the horse was breaking fast, cracked by shock and fear. With me they would possess a lever to use against Kaththea and Kemoc. *They*—who or what were *they?* Who *were* the rulers of this land, and what did they want with us? That the force which had taken me so was not beneficent I was well aware. This was merely another part of that which had tried to trap me in the stone web. And this time I must not summon any aid, lest that recoil upon those I wanted least to harm.

The plain over which we sped did have an end. A dark line of trees appeared to spring out of the ground, so fast was our pace. They were oddly pallid trees, their green bleached, their trunks and limbs gray, as if life had somehow been slowly sucked out of them. And from this gaunt forest came an effluvium of ancient evil, worn and every old, but still abiding as a stench.

THREE AGAINST THE WITCH WORLD

There was a road through that wood, and the stallion's hooves rang on its pavement as if he were shod with steel. It did not run straight, but wove in and out. And now I had no desire to leap from my seat, for I believed that more than just clean death awaited any who touched this leached ground.

On and on pounded my mount. I no longer strove to contact its mind; rather did I husband what strength I possessed in perhaps a vain hope that there would be some second allowed me in which I could use every bit of my talent in a last stroke for freedom. And I tried to develope a crust of my own, an outer covering of despair, so that whatever intelligence might be in command would believe I was indeed now its full captive.

Always I had been one who depended upon action of body more than of mind, and this new form of warfare did not come easily. For some men fear ignites and enrages, it does not dampen nor subdue, and so it is with me. I must now curb my burning desire to strike out, and instead harbor all my ability to do so against a time when I might have at least the smallest of chances.

We came through the wood, but still we kept to the road. Now before us was a city, towers, walls. . . .Yet it was not a city of the living as I knew life. From it spread an aura of cold, of utter negation of my kind of living and being. As I stared at it I knew that once I was borne within those gray walls Kyllan Tregarth as he now was would cease to be.

Not only did my inborn rejection of death arm me then, but also the remembrance of those I had betrayed by my yielding to this enchantment. I must make my move—now!

I struck, deep down, through the vanishing crust, into the will of the thing which had captured me. *My will now*, not to turn, to reach safety for myself, but to avoid what lay before me as the final end. If I would die it would be a death of my choosing.

Perhaps I had played my part so well I had deceived that which would compel me to its own ends, or perhaps

it had no real knowledge of my species. It must have relaxed its strongest force, for I succeeded in part. That
steady stride faltered, and the stallion turned from the
city road. I held to my purpose, despite a boiling up of that
other will. Then came a petulant flash of anger which
reached me almost as if I understood words shouted at
me from the walls now to my left. Very well, if I would
have it so, then it would let me choose—

And in that was a hint of the wearing of age on the
force in command. For, angered by defiance, it was willing to sacrifice a pawn that might be of greater value alive.

The stallion ran smoothly and I had no doubts at all
that I rode to my death. But no man dies tamely and I
would not yield where any chance of a fight remained.
There was a flash in the sky as a bird flapped overhead.
The shimmer about it—Flannan! That same one that had
visited us on the islet? What was its purpose?

It made a sudden dart and the stallion veered, voicing
at the same time a scream of rage, though he did not
abate his pace. Again and again the bird dived, to change
the path of the animal, until we headed north, away from
the city, on ground which climbed to heights forest cloaked and dark against the sky, but green and good, with
none of the withered evil of that other wood.

Once the stallion was headed in this direction the Flannan flew above us, keeping a watchful eye upon our going.
And in me a small, very small hope was kindled, a fire
which a breath could have puffed into nothingness. The
Flannan served good, or at least was an ally, and by so
much had it challenged that other Power in this land. Thus
by a fraction had I the aid of something which might be
well disposed to me.

In my need I strove to communicate with any such unknown friend, using the link sense I shared with those of
my triple birth. But I was not seer trained; I had no hope
of contact. Then I feared lest I endanger those who I
hoped were still safe. Only one short cast did I make be-

fore I busied myself with thoughts of what I could do for myself.

We were running into broken ground, not quite as twisted and torn as the foothills of the western range, but still cut by sharp bitten ravines and craggy outcroppings. It was no country into which one should penetrate at a wild run. When I tried to reach the stallion's consciousness I found nothing now, only the command to run and run which I could not break.

The end came as we reached the top of a rise, where our path was a narrow one between cliffside wall and a drop into nothingness. In that moment my hope was extinguished, for the Flannan made another of those darts, the stallion leaped, and we were falling—

All men speculate sometime during their lives on the nature of death. Perhaps this is not so common while we are young, but if a man is a warrior there is always the prospect of ending at the point of every sword he must face. Thus he cannot push from him the wonder of what will become of that which is truly him, once that sword may open the final gate.

There are believers who hold to them the promise of another world beyond that gate, in which there is a reckoning and payment on both sides of the scale, for the good and the ill they have wrought in their lifetimes. And others select endless sleep and nothingness as their portion.

But I had not thought that pain, torment so racking that it filled the entire world, was what ate on one when life was passed. For I was pain—all pain—a shrieking madness of it in which I no longer had a body, was only fire ever burning, never quenched. Then that passed and I knew that I had a body, and that body was the fuel of the flame which burned.

Later, I could see . . . and there was sky over me, blue as ever the sky of life had been. A broken branch showed a freshly-splintered end against that sky. But always the abiding pain was a cover over and about me, shutting off the reality of branch and sky.

Pain—and then a small thought creeping through the pain, a dim feeling that this was not the mercy of death, that that was yet to come and I had life still to suffer. I closed my eyes against the sky and the branch and willed with all left in me, in that small place yet free from the crowding pain, that death would come and soon.

After awhile there was a little dulling of the pain and I opened my eyes, hoping this meant death was indeed close, for I knew that sometimes there was an end to agony when a man neared his departure. On the branch now perched a bird—not the Flannan, but a true bird with brilliantly blue-green feathers. It peered down at me and then raised its head and gave out a clear call. And I wondered dully if so fair a thing could be an eater of carrion, akin to those black ill-omened gleaners of the battlefields.

The pain was still a part of me, yet between it and me there was a cushioning cloud. I tried to turn my head, but no nerve nor muscle obeyed my will. The sky, the branch, the peering bird: that was what my world had become. But the sky was very blue, the bird was beautiful, and the pain less. . . .

As I had heard the bird call, so now I heard another sound. Hooves! The stallion! But I could not be charmed onto his back now; in that much had I escaped the trap. The pound of hooves on earth stopped. Now came another noise. . . .But that did not matter; nothing mattered—save that the pain was less.

I looked up into a face which came between me and the branch.

How can I describe a dream in clumsy words? Are there ever creatures fashioned of mist and cloud, lacking the solid harshness of our own species? A wraith from beyond that gate now opening for me—?

Pain, sudden and sharp, bore me once more into torment. I screamed and heard that cry ring in my own ears. There was a cool touch on my head and from that spread a measure of curtain once more between me and red agony. I gasped and spun out into darkness.

But I was not to have that respite for long. Once more I came into consciousness. This time neither branch nor bird nor wraith face was over me, though the sky was still blue. But pain was with me. And it exploded in hot darts as there was movement over and about me where someone subjected my broken body to further torment.

I whimpered and begged, my voice a quavering ghost which was not heeded by my torturer. My head was raised, propped so, and forcing my eyes open I strove to see who wished me such ill.

Perhaps it was the pain which made that whole picture wavery and indistinct. I lay bare of body, and what I saw of that body my mind flinched from recording—broken bones must have been the least of the injuries. But much was hidden beneath red mud and the rest was being speedily covered in the same fashion.

It was hard in my dizzy state to see the workers. At least two of them were animals, bringing up the mud with front paws, patting it down in mounds over my helpless and broken limbs. Another had a scaled skin which gave off sparkling glints in the sunlight. But the fourth, she who put on the first layer with infinite care. . .

My wraith? Just as the Flannan's feathered wings had shimmered, so did her body outlines fade and melt. Sometimes she was a shadow, then substance. And whether that was because of my own condition or an aspect of her nature I did not know. But that she would do me well instead of ill I dimly guessed.

They worked with a swift concentration and deftness, covering from sight the ruin of torn flesh and broken bones. Not as one would bury a spirit-discarded body, but as those who labor on a task of some delicacy and much need.

Yet none of them looked into my eyes, nor showed in any way that they knew I was aware of what they did. After a time this came to disturb me, leading me to wonder if I were indeed seeing this, or whether it was all born of some pain rooted hallucination.

It was not until she who led that strange company reached the last packing of mud under my chin and smoothed it over with her hands that she did at last look into my eyes. And even so close a view between us brought no lasting certainty of her true countenance. Always did it seem to flow or change, so that sometimes her hair was dark, her face of one shape, her eyes of one color, and the next she was light of hair, different of eye, changed as to chin line—as if, in one woman, many faces had been blended, with the power of changing from one to another at her will or the onlooker's fancy. And this was so bewildering a thing that I closed my eyes.

But I felt a cool touch on my cheek and then the pressure of fingertips on my forehead growing stronger. There was a soft singing which was like my sister's voice when weaving a spell, and yet again unlike, in that it held a trilling like a bird's note, rising and falling. But from that touch spread a cooling, a soothing throughout my head and then down into my body, putting up a barrier against the pain which was now a dim, far-off thing, no longer really a part of me. And as the singing continued it seemed that I did not lay buried in mud for some unknown reason, but that I floated in a place which had no relation to time or space as I knew those to exist.

There were powers and forces in that place beyond measurement by human means, and they moved about on incomprehensible duties. But that it all had meaning I also knew. Twice did I return to my body, open my eyes and gaze into that face which was never the same. And once behind it was night sky and moonlight, and once again blue, with drifting white clouds.

Both times did the touch and the singing send me out once more into that other place beyond the boundaries of our world. Dimly I knew that this was not the death I had sought during the time of my agony, but rather a renewing of life.

Then for the third time I awoke, and this time I was alone. And my mind was clear as it had not been since that dawn when I had looked at the stallion by the river. My head was still supported so that I could look down my body mounded by clay. It had hardened and baked, with here and there a crack in its surface. But there were no fingers on my flesh, no voice singing. And this bothered me, first dimly and then with growing unease. I strove to turn my head, to see more of where I lay, imprisoned in the earth.

XI

THERE WAS a curving wall to my left, and, a little way from that saucer-like slope, a pool which bubbled lazily, a pool of the same red mud hardened upon my body. I turned my head slowly to the left: again there was the wall and farther beyond another pool, its thick substance churning. It was day—light enough, though there were clouds veiling the sun. I could hear the soft plop-plop as the pool blew bubbles and they broke.

Then came another sound, a plaintive mewling which held in it such a burden of pain that it awoke my own memories, hazy though they now tended to be. On the rim of the saucer something stirred and pulled itself laboriously along. It gathered in a back-arched hump and each movement was so constrained and awkward that I knew the creature was sorely injured.

It slid over the concave slope, uttering a sharp yowl

of hurt. A snow cat! The beautiful gray-white of its thick fur was dabbled with blood. There was an oozing rent in its side, so deep I thought I could see the white of bone laid bare. But still the cat crawled, its eyes fixed on the nearest pool, uttering its plaint. With a last effort of what must have been dying energy it rolled into the soft mud, plastering its hurt and most of its body. Then it lay still, now facing me, panting, its tongue lolling from its jaws, and it no longer cried.

I might have believed the cat dead, save that the heavy panting continued. It did not move again, lying half in the pool of mud as if utterly spent.

My range of vision was very limited; whatever braced my head to give it to me was not high. But I could see other pools in this depression. And by some of them were mounds which could mark other sufferers who had dragged their hurts hither.

Then I realized that all my pain was gone. I had no desire to move, to break the dried covering which immobilized me. For I felt languidly at ease, soothed, a kind of well being flowing through my body.

There were a number of tracks in the dried mud about me, even prints left in that mounded over my body. I tried to see them more clearly. Had it been truth and not a dream, that half-memory of lying here torn and broken while two furred and one scaled creature had worked to pack me under the direction of an ever-changing wraith? But all trace of the latter were missing, save for a hand print which was left impressed, sharp and clear, over the region of my heart.

Slender fingers, narrow palm—yes it was human, no animal pad nor reptile foot. And I tried to remember more clearly the wraith who had been one woman and then another in a bewildering medley of shimmering forms.

The snow cat's eyes were closed, but it still breathed. Along its body the mud was already hardening into a protective crust. How long—for the first time the idea of time itself returned to me. Kaththea—Kemoc! How long had it

been since I had ridden away from them on that devil's
lure?

My languid acceptance broke as the need for action
worked in me. I strove to move. There was no yielding of
the dried mud. I was a helpless prisoner, encased in stone
hard material! And that discovery banished all my waking
content.

I do not know why I did not call aloud, but it never
occurred to me to do so. Instead I used the mind call,
not to those I had deserted during my bewitchment, but
to the wraith, she who might not have any existence at
all save in my pain world.

What would you do with me?

There was a scurry. A thing which glinted with rain-
bow colors skittered across the basin, reared up on hind
legs to survey me with bright beads of eyes. It was not
any creature I had known in Estcarp, nor was it from
one of the legends. Lizard, yes, but more than a mere
green-gold reptile. Beautiful in its way. It had paused at
my buried feet; now it gave a little leap to the mound
which encased me and ran, on its hind legs, up to my
head. There it stopped to examine me searchingly. And I
knew there was intelligence of a sort in its narrow, pike
crested head.

"Greeting, sword brother." The words came out of me
unthinkingly.

It whistled back, an odd noise to issue from that scaled
throat. Then it was gone, a green-gold streak heading up
and over the rim of the saucer.

Oddly enough its coming and going allayed my first
dismay at finding myself a prisoner. The lizard had certainly not meant me harm and neither, I was certain, had
those who had left me here. That was apparent by my
own present feeling of well being, and by the actions of
the sorely hurt snow cat. This was a place of healing to
which an animal would drag itself if it could. And those
virtues had been applied to me . . . by whom? The liz-

111

ard, the furred ones . . . the wraith. . . .yes, surely the wraith!

Though I could not smell sorcery as Kaththea could, I was sure no evil abode here—that it was an oasis of some Power. And I was alive only because I had been brought into its beneficient influence. Now I knew by a tingling of my skin, a prickling of my scalp, a little like that excitement which eats one before the order to advance comes, that there was something on the way.

Several of the lizards sped down the saucer side, and behind them, at a less frantic pace, came two of the furred beasts, their hides also of a blue-green shade. Their narrow heads and plumed tails were those of a tree dwelling animal I knew, but they were much larger than their brothers of Estcarp.

Behind this advance guard and out-scouts she came, walking with a lithesome stride. Her dark hair hung loose about her shoulders—but *was* it dark? Did it glint with a red hue? Or was it light and fair? To me it seemed all that at one and the same time. She wore a tunic of green-blue close-fitting her body, leaving arms and legs bare. And this garment was girdled by a broad belt of green-blue gems set thickly in pale gold, flexible to her movements. About each slender wrist was a wide band of the same gems, and she carried by a shoulder strap a quiver of arrows, all tipped with blue-green feathers, and a bow of the pale gold color.

One could be far more certain of her garments than of her, since, though I struggled to focus on her face and that floating cloud of hair, I could not be sure of what I saw, that some haze of change did not ever hold between us. Even as she knelt beside me that disorientation held.

"Who are you?" I asked that baldly, for my inability to see her clearly irked me.

Amazingly, I heard her laugh. Her hand touched my cheek, moved to my forehead, and under that touch my vision cleared. I saw her face—or one face—sharply and distinctly.

THREE AGAINST THE WITCH WORLD

The features of the Old Race are never to be mistaken: the delicate bones, the pointed chin, the small mouth, larger eyes, arched brows. And she possessed these, making such beauty as to awe a man. But there was also about her a modification which hinted at the unhuman as I knew human. That did not matter—not in the least did it matter.

A warrior knows women. I was no Falconer to foreswear such companionship. But it is also true that some appetites run less deeply with the Old Race. Perhaps the very ancientness of their blood and the fact that the witch gift has set a wedge between male and female makes this so. I had never looked upon any woman whom I wanted for more than a passing hour of pleasure such as the Free Companions of the Sulcar give, finding equal enjoyment of such play. But it was no passing desire which awoke in me as I gazed at that face. No, this was something different, a heightening of the excitement which had built in me as I had sensed her coming, a thing I had never known before.

She laughed and then fell sober once again, her eyes holding mine in a lock which was not quite the communication I wished.

"Rather—who are you?" Her demand was swift, almost roughly spoken.

"Kyllan of the House of Tregarth, out of Estcarp," I replied formally, as I might on delivering a challenge. What was it between us? I could not quite understand. "And you?" For the second time I asked, and now my tone pressed for her reply.

"I have many names, Kyllan of the House of Tregarth, out of Estcarp." She was mocking me, but I did not accept that mockery.

"Tell me one, or two, or all."

"You are a brave man," her silken mockery continued. "In my own time and place I am not one to be lightly named."

"Nor will I do it lightly." From whence had come this word play new to me?

She was silent. Her fingers twitched as if she would lift them from my forehead. And that I feared, lest my clear sight of her be so spoiled.

"I am Dahaun, also am I Morquant, and some say Lady of the Green—"

"—Silences," I finished for her as she paused. Legend—no! She was alive; I felt the pressure and coolness of her flesh against mine.

"So you know me after all, Kyllan of the House of Tregarth."

"I have heard the old legends—"

"Legends?" Laughter bubbled once again from her. "But a legend is a tale which may or may not hold a core of truth. I dwell in the here and now. Estcarp—and where is Estcarp, bold warrior, that you know of Dahaun as a legend?"

"To the west, over the mountains—"

She snatched her hand away, as if the touch burnt her fingertips. Once more distortion made her waver in my sight.

"Am I suddenly made so into a monster?" I asked of the silence fallen between us.

"I do not know—are you?" Then her hand was back, and once more she was clear to see. "No, you are not—though what you are I do not know either. That Which Dwells Apart strove to take you with the Keplian, but you were not swallowed up. You fought in a way new to me, stranger. And then I read you for a force of good, not ill. Yet the mountains and what lie behind them are a barrier through which only ill may seep—or so say *our* legends. Why did you come, Kyllan of the House of Tregarth, out of Estcarp?"

I had no wish to dissemble with her: between us must be only the truth as well as I could give it.

"For refuge."

"And what do you flee, stranger? What ill have you wrought behind you that you must run from wrath?"

"The ill of not being as our fellows—"

"Yes, you are not one but three—and yet, also one. . . ." Her words aroused memory. "Kaithea! Kemoc? What—?"

"What has happened to them since you would go ariding the Keplian, thus foolishly surrendering yourself to the very power you would fight? They have taken their own road, Kyllan. This sister of yours has done that which has troubled the land. We do not easily take Witches to our bosoms here, warrior. In the past that served us ill. Were she older in magic, then she would not have been so eager to trouble dark pools which should be left undisturbed in the shadows. So far she has not met that which she cannot face with her own shield and armor. But that state of affairs will not last long—not here in Escore."

"But you are a Wise One." I was as certain of that as if I saw the Witch Jewel on her breast, yet I also knew that she was not of the same breed as the rulers of Estcarp.

"There are many kinds of wisdom, as you well know already. Long ago, roads branched here in Escore, and we Green People chose to walk in different ways. Some led us very far apart from one another. But also through the years we learned to balance good against ill, so that there was no inequality to draw new witchcraft in. To do so, even on the side of good, will evoke change, and change may awaken things which have long slumbered, to the ill of all. This has your sister done—as an unthinking child might smite the surface of a pool with a stick, sending ripples running, annoying some monster at ease in the depths. Yet . . ." She pursed her lips as if about to give judgment, and in that small movement lost more of the strangeness which separated us, so that I saw her as a girl, like Kaththea. "Yet, we can not deny to her the right of what she has done; we only wish she had done it elsewhere!" Again Dahaun smiled. "Now, Kyllan of Tregarth, we have more immediate things to see to."

Her hand went from my head to the baked clay over

my chest. Down the center of that she scratched a line with the nail of her forefinger, again marking such along my arms and legs.

The creatures that had accompanied her thereupon set to work, clawing away along those lines, working with a speed and diligence which suggested this was a task they had performed many times before. Dahaun got to her feet and crossed to the snow cat, stooping to examine the drying mud, stroking the head of the creature between the eyes and up behind the ears.

Speedy as her servants were, it took them some time to chip me out of my covering. But finally I was able to rise out of the depression which was the shape of my body. My limbs were whole, although scarred with marks of almost healed hurts I would have thought no man could survive.

"Death is powerless here, if you can reach this place," said Dahaun.

"And how *did* I reach this place, lady?"

"By the aid of many strengths, to which you are now beholden, warrior."

"I acknowledge all debts," I said, giving the formal reply. But I spoke a little absently, since I looked down upon my nakedness and wondered if I was to go so bare.

"Another debt also I lay upon you." Amusement became a small trill of laughter. "What you seek now, stranger, you shall find up there."

She made no moved to leave the wounded cat, merely waved me to the saucer's rim. The ground was soft underfoot as I hurried up the slope, a couple of the lizards flashing along.

There was grass here, tall as my knees, soft and green, and by two rock pillars a bundle of nearly the same color. I pulled at a belt which held it together and inspected my new wardrobe. The outer wrapping was a green cloak, within garments which seemed at first well tanned and very supple leather, and which I then decided were some unknown material. There were breeches with attached leg-

116

gings and booted feet sections, the soles soft and earth-feeling. Above the waist I donned a sleeveless jerkin which latched halfway down my chest by a metal clasp set with one of the blue-green gems Dahaun favored. The belt supported not a sword, but a metal rod about as long as my forearm and a finger span thick. If it was a weapon, it was like none I had seen before.

The clothing fitted as if it had been cut and sewn for me alone, and gave a marvelous freedom to my body, such as was lacking in the mail and leather of Estcarp. Yet I found my hands were going ever to feel for the arms I did not wear: the sword and dart gun which had been my tools for so long.

With the cloak over my arm I strode back to the edge of the saucer. Now that I could look down upon it I saw that the area was larger than I had thought. A dozen or more of the mud pools were scattered haphazardly about it, and more than one had a patient immobilized—though all of these were animals or birds.

Dahaun still knelt, stroking the snow cat's head. But now she looked up and waved with her other hand and a moment later arose and came to join me, surveying me with a frankly appraising stare.

"You are a proper Green Man, Kyllan of the House of Tregarth."

"A Green Man?"

It did not seem so difficult now for me to read her features, though I still could not have given a positive name to the color of her hair or eyes.

"The Green People." She pointed to the cloak I held. "Though this is only their outer skin that you wear, and not our true semblence. However, it will serve you for what needs be done." She put her half closed fist to her mouth as had my sister when engaged in sorcery, but the sound she uttered was a clear call, not unlike the high note of a verge horn.

A drumming of hooves brought me around, my hand seeking a weapon I no longer had. Sense told me this was not the stallion that had been my undoing, yet that sound now made my flesh creep.

They came out of the green shadow of a copse, shoulder to shoulder, cantering easily and matching their paces. They were bare of saddle or bridle, but only in that were they like the stallion. For they had not the appearance of true horses at all. More closely allied to the prong-horns, yet not them either, they were as large as a normal mount, but their tails were brushes of fluff they kept clipped tight against their haunches as they moved. There was no mane, but a topknot of fluffy longer hair on the crest of each skull, right above a horn which curved gracefully in a gleaming red arc. In color they were a sleek, roan red, with a creamy underbody. And for all their strangeness I found them most beautiful.

Coming to a stop before Dahaun, they swung their heads about to regard me with large yellow eyes. As with the lizard, they shared a spark of what I realized was intelligence.

"Shabra, Shabrina," Dahaun said gravely in introduction, and those proud horned heads inclined to me in dignified recognition of their naming.

Out of the grass burst one of the lizards, running to Dahaun, who stopped to catch it up. It sped up her arm to her shoulder, settling there in her hair.

"Shabra will bear you." One of the horned ones moved to me. "You need have no fears of *this* mount."

"He will take me to the river?"

"To those who seek you," she replied obliquely. "Fortune attend you—good, not ill."

I do not know why I had expected her to come with me, but I was startled at the suggestion she would not. So abrupt a parting was like the slicing of a rope upon which one's safety depended.

"You—you do not ride with me?"

She was already astride her mount. Now she favored me with one of those long, measuring stares.

"Why?"

118

To that I had no answer but the simple truth. "Because I cannot leave you so—"

"You feel your debt weighing heavily?"

"If owing one's life is a debt, yes—but there is more. Also, even if there was no debt, still I would seek your road."

"To do this you are not free."

I nodded. "In this I am not free—you need not remind me of that, lady. You owe me no debt—the choice is yours."

She played with one of the long tresses of hair hanging so long as to brush the gems of her belt.

"Well said." Plainly something amused her and I was not altogether sure I cared for her laughter now. "Also, I begin to think that having seen one out of Estcarp, I would see more—this sister of yours who may have stirred up too much for all of us. So I choose your road . . . for this time. HO!" She gave a cry and her mount leaped with a great bound.

I scrambled up on Shabra and fought to keep my seat as he lunged to catch up with his mate. Sun broke through clouds to light us, and as it touched Dahaun she was no longer dusky. The hair streaming behind her in the wind was the same pale gold of her belt and wristlets, and she blazed with a great surge of light and life.

XII

THERE WAS a thing loping awkwardly in a parallel course towards us. Sometimes it ran limpingly on three legs, a forelimb held upcurved; again, stumbling and bent over, on two. Dahaun checked her mount and waited for the creature to approach. It lifted a narrow head, showed fangs in a snarl. There were patches of foam at the corners of its black lips, matting the brindle fur on its neck and shoulders, while the forelimb it upheld ended in a red blob of mangled flesh.

It growled, walked stiff-legged, striving to pass Dahaun at a distance. As I rode to join her, my hair stirred a little at skull base. For this was not animal, but something which was an unholy mingling of species—wolf and man.

"By the pact." Its words were a coughing growl and it made a half gesture with its wounded paw-hand.

"By the pact," Dahaun acknowledged. "Strange, Fikkold, for *you* to seek what lies here. Have matters gone so badly that the dark must seek the light for succor?"

The creature snarled again, its eyes gleaming, yellow-red pits of that evil against which all clean human flesh and spirit revolts.

"There will come a time—" it spat.

"Yes, there will come a time, Fikkold, when we shall test Powers, not in small strikes against each other, but in open battle. But it would appear that you have already done battle, and not to benefit for you."

Those yellow-red eyes shifted away from Dahaun, as if they could not bear to look too long at the golden glory she had become. Now they fastened on me. The twisted snarl was more acute. Fikkold hunched his shoulders as if he wished to spring to bring me down. My hand sought the blade I did not wear.

Dahaun spoke sharply. "You have claimed the right, Fikkold; do you now step beyond that right?"

The wolf-man relaxed. A red tongue licked between those fanged jaws.

"So you make one with these, Morquant?" he asked in return. "That will be pleasant hearing for the Gray Ones, and That Which Is Apart. No, I do not step beyond the right, but perchance you have crossed another barrier. And if you make common cause with these, ride swift, Green Lady, for they need all the aid possible."

With a last snarl in my direction, Fikkold went on, staggering, weaving toward the mud pools, his blood-streaming paw pressed tight to his furred breast.

But what he had hinted at, that Kaththea and Kemoc might be in active danger, sent me pounding along his back trail.

"No!" Dahaun pulled up beside me. "No! Never ride so along a were-trail. To follow it straightly leaves your own track open for them. Cross it, thus. . . ."

She cantered in a criss-cross pattern, back and forth across the blood-spotted track the wounded Fikkold had left. And, though I grudged the time such a complicated maneuver cost us, I did likewise.

"Did he speak the truth?" I asked as I drew level with her again.

"Yes, for in this case the truth would please Fikkold." She frowned. "And if they felt strong enough to meet in an open fight with Power such as your sister can shape and mould, then the balance is surely upset and things move here which have not stirred in years upon long years! It is time we knew what or who is aligned. . . ."

She set her hand to her mouth again as she had when she had summoned the horned ones to our service. But no audible sound issued between her fingers. In my head was that sound, shrill, painful. Both our mounts flung high their heads and gave voice to coughing grunts.

I was not too surprised at the shimmer of a Flannan in its bird shape appearing before us. It flapped about Dahaun as she rode. A moment later she looked to me, her face troubled.

"Fikkold spoke the truth, but it is a worse truth than I thought, Kyllan. Those of your blood have been trapped in one of the Silent Places and the thrice circle laid upon them, such as no witch, lest she be more powerful than your sister, may break. Thus can they be held until the death of their bodies—and even beyond—"

I had faced death for myself, and had come to accept the fact that perhaps I had taken the last sword blow.

121

But for Kaththea and Kemoc I would *not* accept this—not while I still breathed, walked, had hands to hold weapons or to use bare. Of this I did not speak, but the resolution filled me in a hot surge of rage and determination. And more strongly was I pledged to this because of my folly and desertion by the river.

"I knew you would feel so," she said. "But more than strength of body, will of mind, desire of heart, will you need for this. Where are your weapons?"

"I shall find such!" I told her between set teeth.

"There is one." Dahaun pointed to the rod which hung as a sword from my borrowed belt. "Whether it will answer you, I know not. It was forged for another hand and mind. Try it. It is a force whip—use it as you would a lash."

I remembered the crackling fire with which the unknown rider had beaten off the rasti, and I jerked the rod from its sling, to use it as she suggested, as if a thong depended from its tip.

There was a flash of fire crackling against the ground to sear and blacken. I shouted in triumph. Dahaun smiled at me across that burned strip.

"It would seem that we are not so different after all, Kyllan of the House of Tregarth, out of Estcarp. So you do not ride barehanded, nor, perhaps, will you fight alone. For that, we must see. But to summon aid will take time, and that runs fast for those you would succor. Also, it will need persuasion such as you can not provide. Thus we part here, warrior. Follow the blood trail, to do what you must do. I go to other labors."

She was at a gallop before I could speak, her horned one keeping a speed I do not believe even the stallion could have equalled. Before me lay the back trail of the werewolf for my guide.

I followed Dahaun's instructions and continued to crisscross those tracks, but at a steady, ground-eating pace. We descended from that high ground into which the stallion had carried me, away from the healthy country. I did not sight that bleached wood, nor the city, unless a distant gray shadow to my left was a glimpse of that, but there were other places Shabra avoided, sometimes leaving the trail to detour about them—a setting of rocks, an off color splotch of vegetation and the like. I trusted to my mount's decision in such matters, for it was plain this part of the country was a stronghold of those forces against which my kind were eternally arrayed.

Shabra slowed pace. I marveled at how far Fikkold had come with his spouting wound. A flock of black winged things arose from a tangle of brush and twisted trees, circled above us, crying raucously.

Whip!

Out of nowhere came that warning. Then I saw Shabra turn his head, and knew that the alarm came from the one who carried me. I gave a sharp jerk to the weapon. A light flash snapped out. One of the black things screeched, somersaulted in the air and fell. The rest broke, flew for a distance, and then reformed with the cunning of an advance guard, to try once more to complete their circle. Three times they attempted that, and each time the lash drove them off, broke their pattern. From the last attack they flew before us, as if determining somewhere on ahead to lay an ambush.

We were still going down slope. Here the grass in the open spaces was coarser and darker than that of the upper country. And in places it was broken and stamped flat as if a host had gone this way. My scout training asserted control. To ride face on into impossible odds was no way to provide help for those I sought. Tentatively I thought this at Shabra.

They know you come. You cannot hide from those who hold this land.

The answer came clearly and promptly. I was ready to accept any help from my mount which he had ready to offer.

His pace had dropped to a walk. He held his head high, his wide nostrils drawing in and expelling the air in audi-

ble sniffs, as if by this sense he could detect what lay ahead.
Abandoning the blood trail which had guided us to this
point, he swung to the right on a course which angled
sharply from the one we had followed.

Along the pillar way. Peace holds there in part,

Shabra's explanation meant nothing to me, but that he
was willing to risk this route did. I could not scent anything in the air, though I strove to. But there was something else—a weight upon the spirit, a darkening of the
mind, which grew as we advanced, until it was a burden
on me.

We came out on the rim of another slope and below
lay open country with, not too far away, the line of the
river. In that plains land was a circle of menhirs, not concentric rings as had been the stone web, but a single
line of rough pillars, two of which had fallen and lay pointing outward. They encircled or guarded a platform of stone
of a slate-blue color. And on that platform were the two
I sought. While outside the ring of menhirs, a motley
pack of creatures crawled, prowled, sniffed. Black blots
of rasti slithered in and out, visible where the grass was
well trampled. Several werewolves paced, sometimes on
four feet, other times erect. The black birds wheeled and
dipped. An armor-plated thing raised a ghastly head and
clawed forefeet now and then. And white blobs of mist
gathered, drifted, thickened and thinned. But all these moved
outside the ring of stones, and they avoided the two which
had fallen outward, leaving a goodly space free about
those as they continued their seige.

From the circle led two paths of pillars, one from the
direction of the river, one marching up the hill to my
right. Of these, many had fallen, some were broken, even
blackened, as if they had been lightning struck.

Shabra trotted to the line near us. Again he began an
in and out advance. Those broken and blackened stones
he leaped or passed with speed; by the others he modi-
fied his pace. But back and forth, in and out, he worked
down to the besieged circle.

Kyllan! Greeting, recognition from the two I sought.

Then: *Take care! To your left—*

There was an upheaval among the watchers, and one of the armored monsters came at a clumsy run. It opened its mouth to puff foul and stinking breath at us. I swished the whip and the lightning curled about the scaled barrel just behind the head. But that did not slow the thing. Next I laid the lash of energy across its head and eyes. It gave an explosive grunt and plowed ahead.

Hold! Not Kemoc nor Kaththea, but Shabra warning.

Under me the horned one bunched muscle, leaped, plowed to a halt by a standing stone. The armored thing came on, to be hurled back as if it had run headfirst into a wall that even its bulk could not breach. Its coughing roar grew louder as it kept on stupidly attempting to reach us. Now some of the other attackers gathered to join it. A wolf-man, striding on two feet, yellow-red eyes cunning and intelligent, rasti a-boil, a drifting blob of mist—

Hold!

I gripped Shabra as tightly with my knees as I could, and kept a left-handed hold on the curve of his neck while I held ready the whip with my right. He made a dart past one of the shattered pillars while I lashed at the mist curling in at us. There was a burst of brilliant fire. The thing, whatever it might have been, ignited from the whip's force. Rasti squalled as it puffed out to catch two of them in its throes.

We were in another of the pools of safety by a standing stone. The space ahead was not too wide, but midpoint there was a fallen pillar, and there gathered rasti and wolf-men. The mist drifted back from any contact with the weapon I carried.

Come—now!

That was Kaththea. She stood on the blue block, her hands to her mouth as she chanted. Though the meaning of what she sang did not reach me, I felt a response in my body, a rising surge of strength. The horned one sprang,

125

breaking into a run. I lashed out on either side, not with any aim, but to clear our path.

I heard growling from a hairy wolf throat. One of the were-things sprang, striving to drag me from Shabra's back. I stiff-armed it, my blow striking, by good fortune alone, beneath its jaw. But it left a dripping slash along my arm. Somehow I managed to cling to both my seat on the horned one and the whip. Then we were within the circle. And outside, the howls of that weird pack arose in a discordant chorus.

Shabra trotted to the blue stone. Kemoc half lay, half sat there, with his back supported by a shrunken pack. His helm was gone, his arm bandaged. And in his hand was the hilt of a sword, its blade broken into a narrow sliver. Kaththea still stood on the stone, her hands now at her breast. She was gaunt, as if from months of ill foraging, her beauty worn to a dying shadow, her spirit so outgoing through its sheath of flesh that I was frightened to look upon her. I slid from Shabra's back and came to them, dropping the whip unknowingly, my hands out to give them all that I had, of my own strength, comfort—whatever they could draw from me.

Kemoc greeted me with a faint, very faint stretch of lips, the merest shadow of his one-time smile.

"Welcome back, brother. I might have known that a fight would draw you when all else failed."

Kaththea came to the edge of the rock and half jumped, half fell into my arms. For a long moment she clung to me, no Wise Woman, no Witch, but only my sister, who had been sorely frightened and yet found the need to put aside that fear. She raised her head, her eyes closed.

"Power." Her lips shaped the word rather than spoke it clearly aloud. "You have lain in the shadow of Power. When—where?" Eagerness overrode her fatigue.

Kemoc stirred and pulled himself up. He was studying me intently from head to foot, his gaze lingering on my chest where the tunic gaped and the just healed scars from my hurts were still plain to read.

"It would seem that this is not your first battle, brother. But—now it would be well to tend to this—" He gestured to the gash the werewolf had opened on my arm. Kaththea pushed away from me with a little cry of concern.

I felt no pain. Perhaps whatever virtue lay in the healing mud held for a while in the bodies of those so treated. For when Kaththea examined the hurt the edges of the wound were closed and I bled no longer.

"Who has been your aid, my brother?" She asked as she worked.

"The Lady of Green Silence."

My sister raised her head and stared at me as one who seeks for signs of jesting.

"She also calls herself Dahaun and Morquant," I added.

"Morquant!" Kaththea seized upon the second of those names. "Of the Green Ones, the forest born! We must know more, we must!" She moved her hands as if wringing speech from silence.

"You have learned nothing?" Far ago now was that night we had wrought magic that Kaththea's spirit messenger might cross time. "What happened? How and why have you come here?"

Kemoc answered first. "As to your first question, we have learned that trouble arises swiftly hereabouts. We left the islet because—" He hesitated, his eyes avoiding mine.

I gave him the rest: "Because you sought one whose folly had made him easy prey for the enemy? Is that not the right of it?"

And he respected me enough not to give any comforting lie.

"Yes. Kaththea—when we awoke, she knew, and through her did I also, that evil had come to you."

Kaththea asked softly, "Had you not thrown open the gate to it when you used your gift in an ill fashion, even if the result was for our good? We knew not how you had been taken from us, only that this was so. And that we must find you."

127

"But the Familiar—you needed to await its return."

She smiled at my protest. "Not so. Where I am, there it will come—though that has not yet happened. We found your trail—or at least a trail of active evil. But where it led"—she shivered—"there we dared not follow—not without such safeguards for our inner selves that I did not have the knowledge to weave. Then those came a-hunting, and we ran before them. But this is a holy place in which that kind can not venture. So we took refuge here, only to discover that we had trapped ourselves, for they have woven their net outside and we are within two walls, one built by the enemy."

Then she sighed and swayed so that I threw out an arm to support her. Her eyes closed and she leaned back against me as Kemoc made plain the rest of their plight.

"I do not suppose, brother, that you carry any food? It has been three days since we have eaten. There was dew on the stone this morning, enough to quench our thirst a little. But water in such small amounts does little for the filling of an empty belly!"

"I won in with this." I touched the whip with my toe. "It can cut us a passage out—"

Kemoc shook his head. "We have not the strength nor the quickness for such a fight now. Also, they have a counterspell to strip Kaththea of all Power if she ventures forth."

But I refused to accept that. "With Kaththea on Shabra, and you and I running—it is worth the try!" But I knew that he was right. Outside the protection of the circle stones we could not out-run and out-fight that pack, now padding, trotting, drifting about, waiting for us to try such desperate measures. In addition both Kemoc and Kaththea had said they were immured here by magic.

"Oh!" In my grasp Kaththea shuddered, shaking as she had on the night she had brought forth the Familiar. She opened her eyes and looked before her with a wide, unseeing stare.

"To the stone with her!" Kemoc cried. "It holds the most virtue in this place."

There was a blanket on the stone, as if perhaps during the night they had rested there together. I swung her pitifully light body up to lie on that, and then scrambled to her side, pulling Kemoc after me. She still moaned a little, her hands moving restlessly back and forth, sometimes lifting up as if she sought to pluck something from the air.

The din which had followed my entrance into the circle had died away. Those creatures paraded in utter silence now, so that Kaththea's small plaints could be heard.

One of those reaching hands caught at Kemoc's scarred fingers, clasped and tightened. His thought sped to me and I took her other hand. We were linked now as we had been on that night.

Expectancy awoke in me. There was a glow in the air above the blue block. The glow grew brighter, formed an image, a winged wand, looking solid and distinct.

For a moment we saw it so, and then, as a dart, it dropped in a streak of white fire. Kaththea's back arched and she gave a great cry, as her messenger returned to that which had given it birth. She was quiet but not silent —not to our minds—for as she learned so did we also, and for us rock, day and world vanished as that knowledge unfolded.

XIII

IT WAS a strange sight we had, operating on two levels. First it was as if we hung in the sky above this land as it had once been, all its fields, woods, streams and mountains spread below us. And it was a fair land then, holding no shadows, no spots of corruption. Also it was a well peopled land, with garths and manors serene and safe. There were three cities—no, four . . . for in the foothills of the mountains was a collection of tall towers apart in use and spirit from the rest. Men and women of the Old Race went about, content and untroubled.

Also there were others, partly of the Old Race, partly of a yet older stock. And these had gifts which led them to be revered. There was a golden light on this land and it drew us as if we rode at twilight through the wind and dark of a coming storm, to see before us the guest lights of a manor wherein dwelt the best of friends. Yes, it drew us, yet we could not accept what it promised, for between us lay the barrier of time.

Then that all encompassing vision narrowed, and we watched the coming of change. There were Wise Women here, but they did not rule so autocratically as they did in Estcarp. For not only did the women of this land have the gift of Power—among them were men who could also walk with spirits.

How did the ill begin? With good intentions, not by any active evil. A handful of seekers after knowledge experimented with Powers they thought they understood. And their discoveries, feeding upon them in turn, altered subtly spirit, mind, and sometimes even body. Power for its results was what first they sought, but then, inevitably, it was Power for the sake of power alone. They did not accept gradual changes; they began to force them.

Years sped as might the moments of an hour. There was the rise of the brother-sisterhood, first secretly, then in the open, dedicated to experimentation, with volunteers, then with those forced to their purposes. Children, animals, things were born which were not as their parents had been. Some were harmless, even of great beauty and an aid to all. But that kind became fewer and fewer. At first those that were distorted, ill-conceived, were destroyed. Then it was proposed that they be kept, studied, examined. Later yet their makers released them, that they might be observed in freedom.

And, as the corruption spread and befouled those who dabbled in it, these monstrosities were used! Nor did the users and the makers any longer place bonds on the fashioning of such dark servants and weapons.

So began a struggle, to eclipse the fast fading brightness of the land. There was a party of the Old Race, as yet unshadowed by the evil flowering among their kind. At first they sounded war horns, gathering a host to put down the enemy. But they had waited far too long; they were as a dipper of water against the ocean. War brought them bitter defeat and the prospect of being utterly lost in the ocean of defilement which was turning their homeland into a morass wherein no decent thing might find existence.

There were leaders who argued that it was better to perish in war than to live under the hand of the enemy, taking with them all that they held dear, so that death would in fact be safety from that which threatened more than the body. And there were many who supported them in that. We watched households go into their manors, take comfort together, and then bring down upon themselves a blotting out by raw forces they deliberately summoned and did not try to control.

But others held to a faith that the end was not yet for them and their kind. Against the array of the Enemy they were a pitifully few in number. But among them were some wielders of the Power such as even their opponents might well fear. And these ordered an ingathering of those willing to try another road.

There was this about the Old Race: they were deeply rooted in their own country, drawing from the land a recharging of energy and life force. Never had they been wanderers, rovers, seekers of the physical unknown—though they moved afar in mind and spirit. And to leave the land was almost as hard as death. Still they were minded to try this. And they set out for the west and what might lie across the bordering mountains there.

They did not go without trouble. The crooked servants of

the Enemy harassed their train, harried them by night and day. They lost men, women, families—some to death, some otherwise. Yet they held to their purpose. Through the mountains they fought their way. And once beyond those barriers, they turned and wrought such havoc against the land that it closed the road behind them for century upon century.

Left to itself, evil boiled and spread out in greedy freedom. But it was not entire master in the land, even though what challenged it lay very low, making no move in those first years to betray its presence. The Old Race had not taken with it any of the creatures that had been born of experimentation, not even those atuned to good rather than ill. A few of these were strong, and they withdrew to the waste spaces and there disguised themselves against detection. There were also those who were not of the Old Race in whole, but part more ancient yet. And these were so united to the land that it was their life base.

There were only a handful of these, yet they were held in awe and shunned by the new rulers. For, though they had not stirred against evil, nor actively aided good, yet they had such forces under their command as could not be reckoned by evil. These too withdrew to the wild, and in time they attracted to them the created ones in loose alliance. But evil ruled totally except in these wastes.

Time flowed as the river current. Those who were drunk with power arose to greater and greater extravagances in its use. Quarreling, they turned upon one another, so that the countryside was wracked with strange and terrible wars, fought with energies and inhuman, demonic things. Struggles lasted so for centuries, but there were drastic defeats, completely wiping out one force or the other. Thus the more outwardly aggressive ate up each other. Then there were those who turned their backs upon the world as it was and ventured farther and farther into weird realms they broke open for exploration. Of these few ever returned. So did the long toll of years bring a measure of quietude to the riven land.

There were still powers of evil, but the majority of them,

satiated by countless tastings and explorations, were lulled
into a kind of abstracted existence in which they floated un-
moved and unmoving. Now those in the wastes ventured
forth, a creeping at first, wary, ready to retreat. For they
only tested evil in small ways, not battles.

In time they held again half the land, always taking
cautiously, never offering direct opposition when one of the
evil ones was aroused to active retaliation. And this had gone
on so long it was the accepted way of life.

Then—into this balanced land we had come, and we saw
in part what our coming had done. Magic summoned magic,
aroused more than one of the dreaming evils into languid
action. Yet against the least of these, alone, we were as helpless as the dust the wind whirls before it. As for now the
evil was old, withdrawn, yet still a little rooted to this plane.
Were we greater than we were—only a little greater—it could
be utterly driven forth into that world, or worlds, which it
now roved, doors sealed behind it, the land free and golden,
and open for our kind once again.

I opened my eyes to meet Kemoc's.

"So now we know," he said quietly. "And are no better for
that knowing. The Council, in our position, could overcome
this. We have not a single chance! And it was—is!—so fair
a land!"

I shared that nostalgic longing for the country we had
seen at the beginning of that time flight. All my life I had
lived under the cloud of war and trouble. And I had faced
from a child the knowledge that I was living in the end days
of a civilization which had no hope. Therefore to have seen
what we had been shown was doubly bitter. And to realize
there was nothing we could do—not even to save ourselves—
was more than bitter.

Kaththea stirred in our hold. Her eyes opened. Tears gathered, flowed to her thin cheeks.

"So beautiful! So warm, so good!" she whispered. "And if—
if we only had the Power—we could bring it back!"

"If we had wings," I said harshly, "we could fly out of

133

here!" I gazed over my shoulder at what lay beyond our protecting ring of stones.

The creatures of the dark still prowled there. And I knew, without needing the telling, they would continue to do so, until there came an end to us and all the slight danger to their overlords which we represented.

It was growing dark and, while I knew that the pillars would keep them at a distance, yet I was also haunted by the knowledge that with the night their true world began, that they would be strengthened by so much. I was hungry and if I felt thus, how much more must Kaththea and Kemoc be in need of food. To stay here, waiting for death—that could not be my way!

Again I thought of Shabra. He had brought me safely in—could he get out again? And doing so, might he serve as a messenger? Could or would Dahaun do aught to aid us now? She had said she was going for help, but hours had passed since then and none had come. It could well be that she had failed in the persuasion she had said she must use. Once more the thought of Kaththea on the horned one, Kemoc and I to flank her in a break out crossed my mind . . . only to be answered by my sister's weak voice:

"Have you forgotten? They have set a witch bar. But you and Kemoc—perhaps that will not encompass you—"

Our combined dissent was quick and hot. As three we would escape or not at all.

"There is no way left to fight them with the Power?"

She shook her head. "Already I have done too much. My acts troubled the quiet here and aroused that which hunts us now. A child playing with a sword cuts itself because it has neither the skill nor strength to use such a weapon properly. There is only this, my brothers: that which sits out there cannot take us. For which we should give thanks, for if it could we would not face clean death of body, but that which is far worse!"

Remembering what I had learned as the stallion bore me towards that city of dread silence, I understood. Yet I was not meant to await death, clean or otherwise, without a struggle. And all I had now was a very faint hope that a wraith girl, who had saved my life and then ridden from me, would redeem a half promise she had made.

I covered my eyes with my hands and strove with every bit of any small power I had to fix upon her face, to somehow reach her, to learn if I could in anyway find hope. For if I could not, then I must turn to some desperate and doubtless fatal move of my own.

But those features of many changes could not be so pinned in mind for a real picture. All the vision faces she had shown me spun elusively, sometimes singly for an instant, sometimes superimposed one on the other. Dahaun was not one of the created ones, produced by a whim of the Old Race; she was one of those who had stood apart, being of yet more ancient blood, and in her the human portion was the lesser.

There was a snort from Shabra. With the coming of evening a pale luminescence fingered up the menhirs. About them swirled threads of light, twining about them as planted vines might seek support on such rough stone. Also the blue platform on which we now rested had its measure of such spectral radiance. By the light I saw the horned one face about, head up, nostrils expanded. Then, with a toss of head so that his red horn caught the light, he voiced a cry, not unlike the challenge of a fighting stallion.

I almost expected to see that black thing which had entrapped me come pacing along with the other besiegers. But Shabra's answer came in another form—a crackle of fire on the crest of the slope down which the line of pillars marched. There was no mistaking its source—the lash of an energy whip!

Dahaun! I put into that silent call all my need.

No answer, save once more the whip cracked, an arc of raw lightning in the sky. A bush flamed where its tip must have struck the ground. And from outside the circle arose a concentrated, growling roar from the things who kept sentry duty there.

Shabra— I reached for contact. *Who rides there?*

Be still! Would you have the Dark Ones know? It was a sharp rebuke.

I was startled. This was no contact with any animal; this was equal chiding equal, or perhaps even an adult rebuking a child. I might have ridden Shabra to this place, but his function was not only that of mount. And now I caught a flash of amusement at my surprise. Then his mind was closed to me as a door might be locked and barred to any entrance.

Kaththea grasped my arm and Kemoc's and pulled herself up.

"There are forces on the move," she said. But something in the curling light about the pillars bedazzled our eyes to anything which lay beyond. We could hear the evil host but we could no longer see it. No more whip cracks broke the night.

"Can you reach—have any contact at all?" Kemoc demanded.

"No, I must not. I could disturb, awaken— Our power is a mixture. Ceremonial magic comes from ritual, from study, used by those who learn as scholars and priestesses. True witchcraft is older, more primitive, allied with nature, not truly bound by our standards of good and evil. In Estcarp we have united the two, but always give the greater weight to magic, not witchcraft. Here magic went utterly wrong and crooked, becoming a twisted, wicked thing. But witchcraft stepped aside and walks in its earlier guise. Thus when I strove to use what I knew I drew magic, yes, but I used a force which had been distorted. What may work in our favor is witchcraft, and of that I have no mastery. Tell me, quickly, Kyllan, of this Lady of Green Silences and how you met with her!"

With my attention half for anything which might move outside the lights of the menhirs, I told my story—and more slowly of what had happened after my awaking in the mud basin.

"Natural forces," Kaththea broke in. "Shape changing—because she has Power which adapts—"

"How do you mean?" I had not guessed that my sister,

never having seen Dahaun, could yet explain some of her mystery.

"The Green Silences—the woodlands—have always had their guardians and inhabitants. And their magic is of wind, water, earth and sky—literally of those. Not as we witches use them, imposing our will for a space, either in illusion or for destruction, but with the rhythm and flow of nature. They will use a storm, yes, but they do not summon one. They can use the rushing current of a river, but within its boundaries. All animals and birds, even plants, will obey them—unless such are already in the service of evil, and thus corrupt. They take on the coloring of their surroundings. If they wish, you can not see them among trees, in water, nor even in the open. And they cannot live among stone walls, nor in places wherein only men dwell, or they wither and die. Because they are of the very stuff of life, so they are feared by the forces of destruction. But also they will be wary of the risking of life. In some ways they are indeed more powerful than we, in spite of all our centuries of magic, yet in others they are more vulnerable. Their like does not exist in Estcarp; they could not make the break to leave this land in which they are rooted. But still we had our legends of their kind—"

"Legends centuries old," I interrupted. "Dahaun—she can not *be* that Lady of those—"

"Perhaps an office descending in some ancient line, the name with it. Morquant is one of the names by which we evoke wind magic, yet you say she gave it as her own. Also, note that unlike a sworn witch she gives you her name freely, proving that she has no fear of so delivering herself into your hands. Only her kind are so above the threat of counterspell."

There was a trill overhead. Startled, we looked up at a blue-green bird such as had been with me during my hours of pain. Three times it circled us, trilling in short bursts of clear, sweet notes. Kaththea gasped, her grip tightening to dig nails into my shoulder, her face becoming even more pale. She whispered:

"They—they are indeed great! I have been—silenced!"

"Silenced?" Kemoc echoed.

137

"I cannot use spells. Should I strive to use an incantation it would not make sense! Kyllan—why? Why would they do this thing? I am now open to what lies out there. Kyllan, they wish us ill, not well! They have chosen this time to stand with evil!"

She pulled away from me and clung to Kemoc. Over her bowed shoulders he gazed hostilely at me, as he had never done before.

Nor could I deny that he might have some cause for such judgment. I had returned to them through the agency of this force which now acted against Kaththea, to take from her what might be her only defense. And I had come charging in blindly, not to bring them any real succor, perhaps merely to direct a final blow. Yet a large part of me would not accept that measurement of what was happening here, even though I could not give any reason for still believing that we had hope for aid.

The prowlers were growing bolder. A lean wolf head was clearly outlined in the light from a menhir; a vast armored paw, talons outspread, waved in another direction. Kaththea raised her head from Kemoc's shoulder. There was now fear in her eyes.

"The lights—look to the lights!"

Until her cry I had not noted the change. When we had awakened from the time spell those wreathing threads had been of a blue shade, akin in color to the rock platform they ringed. Now they were smoky, yellowish, giving one an unpleasant sensation when looked at too closely. That change in them appeared to summon the attackers. More and more faces and paws were visible by their glare. Our besiegers were drawing in closely.

Shabra stamped a forehoof, and the impact on the ground had the thud of hand against war drum, booming unnaturally in the air. Kaththea's throat worked convulsively, as if she were trying to speak; her head turned from side to side, and her hands arose before her by visible effort, as if she struggled against bonds. They jerked, twitched, rebels against her will. And I knew that she was fighting to use her own craft—without avail.

The horsed one began to trot around with the blue stone the core of his circle. His trot became a canter, then sped to a gallop. Now he gave voice in a series of sharp barking cries. Still more faces of evil were plain in the yellow light.

Then I sighted something else, something I had to stare at a long second before I could believe in what my eyes reported. Shabra might not be running on trampled grass, but hock high in a flowing, deep green stream of water. There was a rippling out and away from his circling, gathering impetus as he passed. Not light, nor mist, but a flowing—of what, I could not say. And, under us, the blue stone was growing warm. From its four corners spiraled tendrils of blue which arched over to touch that flowing green, and were swallowed, blue to green. And the green swept on, a little faster, towards the smoky yellow of the pillars. Round and round Shabra galloped.

I dared not watch him, for his circling made me lightheaded. The edge of the green flow lapped at the roots of the menhirs. There followed an explosion of light, as had when my whip had cut at the mist thing. Eyes dazzled, I blinked and rubbed, striving to clear my sight.

Before me the menhirs were no longer a smoky yellow, but each a towering green candle, so lost in light that their rugged outlines vanished. No more did the sentries stare hungrily at us from between them.

The columns began to pulse in waves, as the light mounted higher and higher. But it proved a barrier to our sight of all that lay beyond. We did not see; we heard—a crying, the sound of running. . . . It was the breaking of the siege! I got to my feet, jumped from the platform, sought for the whip I had dropped hours earlier.

Magic, perhaps not that which we knew, but still magic, had come to our aid. Whip in hand I strained to see beyond the pillar light.

"Dahaun!" I did not shout, I whispered, but that I would be answered I was almost sure.

XIV

THEY APPEARED suddenly between two of the candled men-hirs—not as if they had ridden into view, but flashed from the air itself. No longer was Dahaun blonde or dusky; her hair flowed as green as the flood about Shabra's hooves, her skin had a verdent caste, and the others with her were of a like coloring.

They swung whip stocks idly, the flashing lashes not in evidence. But Dahaun carried her bow, strung and ready for action. Now she fitted arrow to string, aimed skyward, and shot.

We did not see the passing of that, but we heard the sound, for it sang, almost as had the bird earlier, up and up, over our heads, its call growing fainter as if vanishing into the immensity of the night sky, never to return. Then, from some lofty point, there burst a rain of fire, splashing in green glitter widely between us and the real stars, and these flakes drifted down, glimmering as they fell. Still those three sat their mounts, gazing soberly at us.

Those who accompanied Dahaun were both men, human to the most part, save that among the loose curls on their temples showed curved horns, not as long or as arching as those on their mounts, and of an ivory shade. They wore the same clothing as she had brought to me at the mud basin, but their cloaks were hooked on their shoulders and swung out behind them.

There was none of that flickering instability about their

140

features which Dahaun possessed, but a kind of withdrawn, almost chilling expression, freezing masculine beauty into a rigidly aloof pattern to put a barrier between us.

Come! Her summons was imperious, demanding.

That was what part of me wanted. But older ties held. I turned and reached out a hand to Kaththea. Then they stood beside me, my brother and sister, facing those others who made no move to pass between the menhirs to us. In a flash I knew without being told that they could not—that what made this a place of refuge for us locked them out.

One of Dahaun's companions snapped his whip impatiently, and sparks crackled in the air.

"Come!" This time she called the summons aloud. "We have little time. That which prowls is routed only for a space."

With my arm about my sister's shoulders, Kemoc on her other side, I walked towards them. Then I saw that Dahaun's eyes were not for me any more; they were on Kaththea, and that between those two met and mingled a current.

Dahaun leaned forward on her horned one. She had shouldered her bow and now one hand came fully into the green glow. With deliberation her fingers moved, outlining a pattern which continued to shine as lines in the air. Kaththea's arm raised by vast and wearying effort which I shared through contact. Quickly I willed strength to her, as did Kemoc. Her fingers spread slowly, so slowly, but in turn she sketched lines—lines which burned blue after the fashion of the block behind us, not green like those of Dahaun.

I heard a quick exclamation from one of Dahaun's escorts.

"Come—sister—" The hand with which she had sketched that sign Dahaun now held out to Kaththea. And I heard a small sigh of relief from my sister.

We passed between the green-lit stones, feeling a tingling throughout our bodies. Small sparks flashed from our skins. I sensed a stir on my scalp as if my hair moved from its roots. Then Dahaun's hand clasped tight about my sister's.

"Give her up to me!" she ordered. "We must ride, and swiftly!"

I mounted then on Shabra, Kemoc behind me. Ride we

did. Dahaun went first, her horned one skimming the ground at a pace which seemed to say that a double rider burden was nothing. The came Kemoc and I, and the two whip swinging guards behind us.

As we left the blazing menhirs a kind of greenish haze accompanied us, and in a measure, at least for me, walled off clean sight of the countryside through which we traveled. Though I strained to see better, I could not sight more than would be visible to a man caught in a fog. And at last I gave up, knowing we must depend wholly upon Dahaun.

There was no uncertainty about her riding. And the first pace she set did not slacken. I began to marvel at the stamina of her horned mounts.

"Where do we go?" asked Kemoc.

"I do not know," I answered.

"It can be that we ride into yet deeper trouble," he commented.

"And maybe we do not! There is no evil in these—"

"Still I do not believe that those now riding rear guard look upon us with much favor."

"They came to save us."

But he was right. Dahaun had brought us out of the refuge which was also a prison; in that much she had favored us. But we could not be sure of what lay ahead.

Though I could not see our path, I believed we were headed back for the heights where lay the healing basin and perhaps the homeland of those who rode with us.

"I do not like to go thus blindly," Kemoc said. "But I do not think they use this screen to confuse *us*. This is a land through which we must feel our way, blinded by ignorance. Kyllan, if we have upset the balance of peace, what must we answer for—beyond our own lives?"

"Perhaps a world!" Yet looking back through time I could not see wherein we might have altered anything we had done, given no more foreknowledge than we held when we rode out of deserted Estford.

I heard a soft laugh from my brother. "Very well, make it a world to be succored, Kyllan. Did not our parents go up against the Kolder blindly and with only the strength within them? Can we reckon ourselves less than they? And we are three, not two. It is in my mind, brother, that we ride now to a hosting—and with such company as shall suit us well."

On and on we rode, and within the envelope of haze perhaps time as well as space was distorted. Yet I thought that outside that the night passed.

The mist began to fade slowly. Trees, brush, outcrops were more visible in it. And they were illumined by dawn light. Then there came a time when the first rays of the sun were bright as we rode into a pass between two crags. Beneath the hooves of the horned ones was a leveled road. And, on either hand, set into the rock walls of the cut, were symbols which looked vaguely familiar to me, but which I could not read. But I heard a small hiss from Kemoc at my back.

"Euthayan!"

"What?"

"A word of power—I found it among the most ancient screeds at Lormt. This must be a well guarded place, Kyllan— no hostile force can pass such safety devices."

The rows of those symbols ended; we were descending again and before us opened a wide basin, well wooded, yet with open glades too, and a silver river in a gentle curve along its bottom. At first glimpse my heart pounded. This was a small slice of that golden ancient land before the coming of ill to twist and foul it. There was that in the air which we drew into our lungs, in the wind which reached us, in all our eyes feasted upon, which soothed, heartened, turned ages back to an untroubled time of joy and freedom when the world was young and man had not yet sought that which would lead to his own undoing.

Neither was it an empty world. Birds of the blue-green plumage, shimmering Flannan, and others sailed above us. I saw two of the lizard folk sitting on top of a stone, their claw hands holding food, watching us as we passed. Horned ones without riders grazed in glades. And over it all was an aura of rightness such as I had never known in all my life.

We had slacked pace as we came through the corridor of

the symbol signs, and now we ambled. Flowers bloomed along the edge of our road, as if gardeners kept that brilliant tapestry of verge. Then we entered an open space near the river, and saw the manor hall.

But this was no building—it was growth out of the soil, alive to shelter the living. Its walls were not quarried stone, nor dead, shaped timber, but trees or strong, tall brush of an unknown species, forming solid surfaces over which grew vines, flowers, leaves.

There was no defense wall, no courtyard. Its wide entrance was curtained by vines. And the roof was the most eye-catching of all, for it arose sharply to a center ridge, the whole thatched with feathers—the blue-green feathers of the birds we had already seen.

We dismounted and the horned ones trotted away on their own concerns, first down to the stream to drink. Dahaun set her arm about my sister's shoulders, drew and supported Kaththea to the doorway. We followed, more than a little wearied, in her wake.

Beyond the vine curtain was a hall, carpeted with tough moss. Screens, some woven of feathers and others of still flowering vines, cut the space about the walls into various alcoves and compartments. And there was a soft green light about us.

"Come—" One of the guards beckoned to Kemoc and me. Dahaun and Kaththea had already disappeared behind a screen. We went in the opposite direction and came to a place where the floor was hollowed out in a pool. Its water was thick and red, and I recognized the scent of it. These far more liquid contents were akin to the healing mud of the basin. Eagerly I stripped, Kemoc following my example. Together we sank into the stuff which drew all aches and pains from us, leaving us languid.

Then we ate, drowsily, of substances set before us in polished wooden bowls. Finally, we slept, on couches of dried moss. And I dreamed.

Here again was a golden land, not this into which our rescuers had brought us, but that earlier and wider territory

144

at which we had looked through the eyes of the Familiar. And there stood manors in that land which I knew with an imtimacy which could belong only to one who had lived within their walls. I rode in company with other men, men who wore faces which I knew— Borderers from the Estcarp mountains, men of the Old Race with whom I had feasted in the rare intervals when there was no active war, and even men and women I had known at Etsford.

And, in the strange manner of dreaming when many things may be mingled, I was sure that the past and the present had become one, that the threats which had been with me since my birth did not hold here, but that once more our people were strong, able, unbeset by those who would drag them and their whole civilization down into the dust of ending.

But with me also was a shadowy memory of a great trial and war which lay behind, and which we had survived through struggle and many defeats, to this final victory. And that dark war had been worth all it had cost, for what we had come to hold.

Then I awoke, and lay blinking at dusky shadows over my head. Yet I carried with me something from that dream, an idea which held the improbability of most dream action, yet which was very real to me, as if in my sleep some geas past my avoiding had been laid on me. As perhaps it had, for in this land were there not forces at work past our divining? I was sure in that hour as to what I must do—as if it were all action past, already laid out in words on some scroll of history.

Kemoc still lay on the neighboring couch, his face clear and untroubled in his sleep. For a moment I envied him, for it seemed that he was under no compulsion such as now moved me. I did not wake him, but dressed in the fresh clothing my host or hostess had left, and went past the screen, into the main hall.

Four of the lizards sat about a flat stone, their slender claws moving about tiny carved objects, no doubt playing a game. Their heads all turned at my coming and they favored me with those unwinking stares of their kind. And two others also looked to me. I raised my hand in a small salute of greeting to her who, sat cross-legged on a wide cushion, a cup by her hand on a low table.

"Kyllan of the House of Tregarth, out of Estcarp." She made that both formal greeting and introduction. "Ethutur of the Green Silences."

He who was with her got lightly to his feet. He was as tall as I, his dark eyes meeting mine on a level. He wore the jerken and breeches like mine, but, as with Dahaun, he had gemmed wristlets and belt in addition. His horns were longer, more in evidence, than those of the guards who had ridden with us from the menhir ring, but save for those he might have been any man of the Old Race. As to his age, I could make no guess. For he might have had a few more years than I counted, but meeting his eyes and what lay behind them, that I doubted. Here was one who had all the unobtrusive authority of he who has commanded men—or forces—for years, who had made decisions and ordered them, or carried them out for himself, abiding by the result without complaint or excuse. This was a leader such as I had known in Koris of the Axe, or my father, little as I could remember of Simon Tregarth.

His eyes measured me in return. But I had stood for appraisement before, and this was not as important to me as that which had carried over from my dream.

Then his hands came out, palm up. Without knowing the why of that gesture, mine moved to them, palm down, our flesh so meeting. Between us passed something else, not as strong a contact as I had with Kemoc and Kaththea, but some of that union. And in that I knew he accepted me—to a point.

Dahaun gazed from one to the other of us; then she smiled. Whether that was in relief as to how our meeting had gone, I could not tell, but she motioned me to another cushion, and poured golden liquid from a flagon into a cup for me.

"Kaththea?" I asked before I drank.

"She sleeps. She will need rest, for more than her body is tired. She tells me that she did not accept the oath of the Witches, but certainly she cannot be less than they. She has

146

the Right, the Will, and the Strength to be a Doer rather than a Seeker."

"If she uses it rightly," Ethutur said, speaking for the first time.

I gave him a level glance across the rim of my goblet. "She has never used it wrongly."

Then he, too, smiled, and the lighting of his general somberness made him indeed a youth and not a war leader of too many strained years. "Never as you fear I meant," he agreed. "But this is not your land—the currents here are very swift and deep, and can be disastrous. Your sister will be the first to admit, when she knows it all, that a new kind of discipline must be exercised. However. . . ." He paused, and then smiled again. "You do not really realize what your coming means to us, do you? We have walked a very narrow path between utter dark on one hand, and chaos on the other. Now forces are loosed to nudge us into peril. Chance may dictate that such a move will bring us through to new beginnings—or it may be the end of us. We have been weighing one fortune against another this day, Kyllan. Here in this valley we have our safety, hardwon, nursed through centuries. We have our allies—none to be despised—but we are few in number. Perhaps the enemy is also limited, but those who now serve them as hands and feet muster the greater."

"And what if your numbers were increased?"

He took up his cup from the table. "In what manner, friend? I tell you this, we do not recruit from other levels of existence! That was the root of all our present evils."

"No. What if your recruits be men of the Old Race—already seasoned warriors—what then?"

Dahaun moved a little on her cushion. "Men can be swayed by the Powers here—and what men do you speak of? All dwelling in Escore made their choice long ago. The handful who chose to stand with us are already one, our blood long since mingled so there is no pure Old Race to be found."

"Except in the west."

Now I had their full attention, though their faces were impassive, their thoughts well hidden from me. Was I indeed bewitched that a dream could possess me after this fashion? Or had I been granted a small bit of foreknowledge as a promise—and bait?

"The west is closed."

"Yet we three came that way."

"You are not of the fullblood either! Paths not closed to you might be closed to others."

"With a guide to whom such paths were open a party could win in."

"Why?" The one word from Ethutur was a bleak question.

"Listen—perhaps you do not know how it is there. We, too, have walked a narrow path such as yours . . ." Swiftly I told them of the twilight of Estcarp and what it would mean to all those who shared my blood.

"No!" Ethutur brought down his fist with such force on the top of the table that the goblets jumped. "We want no more witches here! Magic will open doors to magic. We might as well cut our own throats and be done with it!"

"Who spoke of Witches?" I asked. "I would not seek out the Wise Ones—my life would be forfeit if I did so. But those who carry shields in Estcarp's service are not always one in thought with the Council. Why should they be, in their hearts, when the Witches close so many doors?" And once again I laid facts before them. That marriages were few since women with the Power did not easily lay aside their gift, and births even fewer. That many men went without woman or home-place for all of their lives, and that this was not a thing which made for contentment.

"But if there is a war, they will have assigned their loyalty and you could not find followers," Ethutur objected. "Or those you could find would not be men to whom you could trust your unarmed back—"

"Now there may be an end to war—for a time. Such a blow as was dealt to Karsten in the mountains would also prove a shock to Alizon. I will not know unless I go to see."

"Why?" This time the question was Dahaun's, and I made frank answer.

"I do not know why I must do this, but that I am under

geas, of that I am sure. There is no turning for me from this road—"

"Geas!" She rose and came to kneel before me, her hands tight upon my shoulders as if she would hold me past all escape. Her eyes probed into mine, a kind of searching deeper than that Ethutur had used, deeper than I had thought possible. Then she sat back on her heels, loosing her grasp.

Turning her head she spoke to Ethutur. "He is right. He is under geas."

"How? This is clear land!" Ethutur was on his feet, staring about him as one who seeks an enemy.

"The land is clear; there has been no troubling. Therefore it must be a sending. . . ."

"From whence?"

"Who knows what happens when a balance swings? That this has happened we cannot question. But—to bear the burden of a geas is not easy, Kyllan of the House of Tregarth out of Estcarp."

"I did not believe that it would be so, lady," I replied.

XV

WE MIGHT be riding across a deserted land, we who had been harried and hunted before. No sign of that frightening crew that had besieged us in the menhir-guarded refuge showed; even their tracks had vanished from the soil. Yet I sensed our going was noted, assessed, perhaps wondered over, and this was only a short lull with very false peace.

Ethutur's men rode at my back, and, beside me, against my

wishes, Dahaun who had taken no discouraging from that journey. Before us were the western mountains and the gateway between the lands.

We did not talk much—a few surface words now and then as she pointed out some landmark, either as a guide or a thing to beware in crossing the country, with always an unspoken assurance that I would return to have need of such information. But as I rode my own confidence was not as great. I was a man under compulsion—the way of it I did not understand. Because I would not have Kemoc and Kaththea join their fates to mine in this perilous business I had ridden while they still lay in healing slumber.

That night we camped among trees which were not as fine or tall as those of the Green Valley, but were of the same species, thus friendly to those with me. This time I did not dream—or at least not to remember—yet with my morning waking the need for going was more deeply rooted, spurring me to speed. Dahaun rode on my right and this time she sang, soft and low, and now and then she was answered, by the green birds, or by Flannan in bird form.

She looked at me from the corners of her eyes and then smiled.

"We have our scouts also, man of war. And, even though they know their duty well, it sometimes goes even better if they are alerted. Tell me, Kyllan, what chances have you on this man quest of yours?"

I shrugged. "If matters rest as they did when I fled Estcarp, very few. But with an end made to any Karsten invasion, perhaps that has changed."

"You have those who will come to your horn—your own shield men?"

I was forced to shake my head. "I have no shields pledged to me as overlord, no. But the Borderers among whom I served are landless and homeless. Years ago they were thrice horned as outlaws in Karsten and escaped with only their lives and the bare steel in their hands. Odd, when we came hither we spoke of that—that this would be a land won by swords."

"By more than swords," she corrected me. "However, these

150

landless warriors might well be reckless enough to follow such a quest. In the final saying most of us seek a place to set roots and raise house trees. Here they will pay sword weight instead of tribute. Yet—your seeking is based on guesses, Kyllan, and guesses are light things."

I would not look at her now. I had no dispute for what she said, and the closer we drew to a time of parting the more I rebelled against the invisible purpose which had been laid upon me. Why me? I had no power to command respect, no gift of words such as Kemoc could summon upon occasion. My position as eldest son of Tregarth was nothing to draw any support to my shield. Nor had I made a war name to gather any followers. So—why must I be driven back to a fruitless task?

"To break a geas . . ." Had she been reading my mind? For a second I resented, was ashamed of, what she might have picked from my thought.

"To break a geas, that is courting complete disaster."

"I know!" I interrupted her roughly. "And it can recoil on more than he who breaks it. I ride to the mountains, not from them, lady."

"But not in any helpful spirit." Her tone was a little cold. "Right thinking can draw good fortune, and the reverse is also true. Not that I believe you have any easy path. Nor do I understand why . . ." Her voice trailed into silence. When she spoke again her words were pitched lower, hurried. "I do not know what force can aid beyond the mountains. You leave those here who have reason to wish you well, would will what they can in your behalf. If you fall into danger—think on that, and on them. I can promise you nothing, for this is an untried, unmarked wilderness. But what can be done in your behalf, that I promise will be! And with your sister and brother—who knows indeed!"

She began to talk then of little things which were far apart from my purpose, things which opened for me small sunny vistas of her life as it had been before we came to break the uneasy peace of Escore. It was as if she took me by the hand and welcomed me into the great hall of her life, showing me most of its private rooms and treasures. And that was a gift beyond price, as I knew even as I accepted it, for now she was not the awesome controller of strange powers, but instead, a girl as my sister had been before the Wise Ones rift her from us and strove to remodel her into their own pattern.

Then in turn Dahaun coaxed memories from me. I told her of Etsford and our life there, more of that than of the hard years which followed when we rode mailed and armed about the grim business of war. And the sweet of those memories, even though it carried always a hint of bitter, relaxed me.

"Ah, Kyllan of the House of Tregarth," she said, "I think we two understand each other a little better. And that is to your liking, is it not?"

I felt the warmth of blood-flush rising up throat and cheek. "I cannot hide all thoughts, lady—"

"Is there a need to?" Her question was sober enough, yet under that soberness lurked amusement. "Has there been any need to since first we looked, really looked upon one another?"

She was not bold; it was fact she stated. Then there roused in me such fire that I clenched fists, fought myself, lest I reach for her in the instant, the need to have her in my arms nearly breaking all control. But that would be the false step, the wrong path for both of us. How did I reckon that? It was like the geas, knowledge out of nowhere yet not to be denied. And the hatred of my task grew with that constraint so holding me now.

"Yes—and yes—and yes!" she burst out, equalling my own inner turmoil. "Tell me—make me see what path you shall take when you leave us!" Thus she tried to cut that too taut cord between us.

I sought my memories of our trip over the mountains, recalling it all for her.

"You will be afoot in a wilderness." Dahaun put that into words as if it presented a problem for careful consideration.

I wore Kemoc's mail and helm, and carried his dart gun—though ammunition for that was near exhaustion. My sword and gun had been lost in their flight after leaving the river islet. Yes, I would be afoot and poorly armed in rough wilderness on the other side of the mountain. But how to better that position I could not see.

"Perhaps this is a test for us, to see how well any influence can cross the barrier." Dahaun flung back her head and trilled, her voice echoing. The ground eating pace of the horned ones had brought us very close to the climb to the heights.

A green bird planed down with hardly a beat of its wide wings. It chirped an answer and arose, on beating pinions, higher and higher, heading west. We watched it until it was beyond sight, yet Dahaun still glanced from time to time in its wake. Suddenly she gave a little cry of triumph.

"No barrier to that one! It is over the pass, winging out beyond. Now let us see if it can do anything more."

There came a moment, not too much later, when I swung down from Shabra's back, before me the trail out of Escore. Dahaun did not dismount, nor did her guard. But those sat a little apart, leaving us to a shared silence we dared not break. Then she raised her hand as she had done in her first meeting with Kaththea and sketched a burning symbol in the air. It blazed, dazzling my eyes, so that her features again shifted and changed, as they had not for many hours past.

And I brought my fist up as I would salute a war leader, before I swung around and began that climb with a burst of speed, aware that if I hesitated, or looked behind me, I would break. And that was not to be thought on, for all our sakes.

Nor did I look back as long as I thought I might see anything of Escore to lay ties upon me. But before I set out on the perilous swing across the tree limb valley, I took my last glance at this lost world, as one does when going into exile. I had not felt so torn when we had left Estcarp; this was different. But the mist curtain was closed, I could see nothing, and for that I was very glad.

I spent the night among the mountain rocks, and with the day began the descent up which Kemoc and I had brought Kaththea blindfolded. It was easier, that descent, since now I had only myself to think on. But I did not welcome traveling the broken lands on foot. There was a need to make plans. Those to whom I might appeal had been in camp on the plains when I set forth on my ride to join Kemoc at Etsford, but there was no reason to think that they would still be where I left them.

No Falconer would be tempted by what I had to offer. They lived for fighting, yes, supplying mercenaries for Estcarp and marines for the Sulcar ships. But they were rooted in their Eyrie in the mountains, wedded to their own warped customs and life. There would be no place for them in Escore.

Sulcarmen never ventured too far from the sea which was their life; they would be lost where no surf roared, no waves battered high. I had hopes only of the Old Race uprooted in the south. A few, very few, of the refugees from Karsten had been absorbed into Estcarp. The rest roved restlessly along the border, taking grim vengeance for the massacre of their blood. It had been close to twenty-five years since that happening, yet they would not forget nor really make one with Estcarp dwellers.

Karsten would never be theirs again. They had accepted that. But if I could offer them land of their own, even if they must take it by sword—I believed they might listen. It remained now to find them, and not *be* found by those who would deliver me forthwith to the justice of the Council.

I climbed the ridge from which I had sighted the campfires of those who had hunted us, and waited there until night fell, watching for any trace of continued sentry go there. But the land was dark, although that did not necessarily mean that it was unpatrolled. Kaththea's ruse with the Torgians—how well had that served us? I shrugged. Magic was no weapon for me. I had my gun, my wits, and the training drilled into me. With the morning I must put all to the test.

Even in the last rays of the sun and well into twilight I found myself watching for the bird Dahaun had dispatched across the mountains. Just what service that could perform I had no idea, but just seeing it would have meant much in that hour. But all the flying things I sighted were common to the land, and none flashed emerald.

154

In the early morning I started along the same trail which had brought us into that twisted land. Though I wanted to hasten, yet I knew the wisdom of checking landmarks, of not becoming entangled in the maze. So I went slowly, nursing my water bottle's contents and the supplies Dahaun had provided. Once I was trailed for a space by an upland wolf. But my gift held so that I suggested hunting elsewhere and was obeyed. That disorientation of sight which had been troubling when we had come this way was no longer a problem, so perhaps it only worked when one faced the east, not retreated from it.

I advanced upon the campfire sites, utilizing every scouting trick I knew. The fire scars were there, as well as the traces of more than a company of men, but now the land was empty, the hunters gone. Yet I went warily, taking no risks.

Two logs close together gave me a measure of shelter for the second night. I lay unable to sleep for a while, striving to picture in my mind a map of the countryside. Kemoc had guided us this way, but I had studied as I rode, making note of landmarks and the route. Hazy as I had been, I thought that I would have no great difficulty in winning westward to country where I would know every field, wood, and hill. Those were the fringe lands of deserted holdings where the dwindling population no longer lived, and where I could find shelter.

It came to me through the earth on which my head rested —a steady pound of hoof beat. Some patroller riding a set course? There was only one rider. And I lay in thick cover which only ill luck would lead him to explore.

The approaching horse neighed and then blew. And it *was* heading directly for my hiding place! At first I could not accept such incredible ill fortune. Then I squirmed out of my cramped bed and wriggled snakewise to the right; once behind brush, I got to my feet, my dart gun drawn. Again the horse nickered, something almost plaintive in the sound. I froze, for it had altered course, was still pointed to me, as if its rider could see me, naked of any cover, vividly plain in the moonlight!

155

Betrayed by some attribute of the Power? If so, turn, twist, run and hide as I would, I could be run down helplessly at the desire of the hunter. So being, it would be best to come into the open and face it boldly.

There was a rustling, the sound of the horse moving unerringly towards me, with no pretense of concealment. Which argued of a perfect confidence on the part of the rider. I kept to the shadow of the bush but my weapon was aimed at where the rider would face me.

But, though it wore saddle and bridle, and there was dried foam encrusted on its chest and about its jaws, the horse was riderless. Its eyes showed white, and it had the appearance of an animal that had stampeded and run in fright. As I stepped into the open it shied, but I had already established mind contact. It had bolted in panic, been driven by fear. But the cause of that fear was so ill defined and nebulous I could not identify it.

Now the horse stood with hanging head, while I caught the dangling reins. It could, of course, be part of a trap—but then I would have encountered some block in its mind, some trace, even negatively, of the setting of the trap. No, I felt it was safe, the four feet I needed to make me free of the country and give me that fraction more of security in a place where safety was rare.

I led it along, traveling to the south, and in it was a desire and liking for my company as if my presence banished the fear which had driven it. We worked our way slowly, keeping to cover, so setting some distance between us and the place to which the horse had come as if aimed. And all the time I kept mind contact, hoping to detect any hint if this was a capture scheme.

Finally I stripped off the saddle and bridle, put field hobbles on the horse and turned it loose for the rest of the night, while with the equipment I took cover in heavy brush. But this time I pillowed my head on the support of a saddle and tried to solve the puzzle of whence and why had come what I needed most—a horse. My thoughts kept circling back to Dahaun's winged messenger, and, improbable as it seemed,

I could accept the idea that this was connected. Yet there had been no memory of a bird in the horse's mind.

My new mount was not by any means a Torgian, but its saddle was the light one of a border rider and there was intricate crest set into the horn in silver lines. Sulcar crests were simple affairs, usually heads of animals, reptiles, birds or mythical creatures out of legend. Falconers, recognizing no families, used only their falcon badges with a small under-modification to denote their troop. This could only be the sign of one of the Old Race Houses, and, since such identification had fallen into disuse in Estcarp, it meant that this horse gear was the possession of one of those I sought, a refugee from Karsten.

There was an extremely simple way of proving the right-ness of my guess. Tomorrow morning I need only mount the animal I could see grazing in the moonlight, set in its mind the desire to return whence it had come and let it bear me to its master. Of course, to ride into a strange camp on a missing mount would be the act of a fool. But once in the vicinity of such a camp the mount could be turned loose as if it had only strayed and returned and I could make contact when and if I pleased.

Simple, yes, but once at that camp what brave arguments would I use? I perhaps a total stranger to all therein, striving to induce them to void their allegiance to Estcarp and ride into an unknown land on my word alone—the more so if they rode as blind as Kaththea had had to do! Simple to begin, but impossible to advance from that point.

If I could first contact men I knew, they might listen even if the fiat of outlawry had gone out against me. Men such as Dermont, and others who had served with me. But where to find them now in all the length of the south border country? Perhaps I could fashion a story to serve me in the camp from which the horse had come, discover from the men there where I could meet with my own late comrades.

No battle plan can be so meticulous that no ill fortune can not upset it. As small a thing as a storm-downed tree across a trail at the wrong time may wipe out the careful work of days, as I well knew. The "lucky" commander is the one who can improvise on a moment's notice, thus pulling victory out of the very claws of defeat. I had never commanded more than a small squad of scouts, nor had I before been called upon to make a decision which risked more than my own life. How could I induce older and more experienced men to trust in me? That was the growing doubt in my mind as I tried to sleep away the fatigue of the day, be fresh for the demands of the morrow.

Sleep I did, but that was a troubled dozing which did not leave me much rested. In the end I took my simple solution: work back to the camp from which the horse had come, free the animal without being seen, scout to see who might be bivouacked there. And that I did, turning the horse south at not more than a walking pace. One concession to caution I made: we kept to the best cover possible, avoiding any large stretch of open. Also I watched for green against the sky. Still haunting me was that thought—or was it a hope?—that Dahaun's messenger might be nearby.

We had left Estcarp in late summer, and surely we had not been long away, yet the appearance of the land and the chill in the air was that of autumn. And the wind was close to winter's blast. In the day I could now see the purple fringe of the mountains. And—nowhere along that broken fringe of peaks did I sight one that I could recognize, though I had studied that territory for most of my life. Truly the Power had wrought a great change, one such as stunned a man to think on. And I did not want any closer acquaintance with a land which had been so wrung and devastated.

But it was south that the horse went, and it was not long before we came into the fringe lands. Here there were raw pits in the earth from which upthrust the roots of fallen trees, debris of slides, and marks of fire in thick powdery ash. I dismounted, for the place was a trap in which a mount could easily take a false step and break a leg. And once, on impulse, I put my hand to a puddle of that ash, wind-gathered into a hollow, and marked my forehead and chest with a very old sign. For one of the guards against ill witchcraft was ash from honest wood fire, though that was a belief I had never put to test before.

The horse flung up its head and I caught its thought. This was home territory. Straightaway I loosened my hold on the reins, slapped the animal on the rump and bade it seek its master . . . while I slipped into a tangle of tree roots, to work my way stealthily to the top of a nearby ridge.

XVI

WHAT I SAW as I lay belly flat on the crest of the slope was no war camp. This was centered by a shelter built not for a day nor a week's occupancy, but more sturdily, to last at least a season—a stockade about it. Though that safeguard was not yet complete—logs were still waiting to be upended and set into place to close its perimeter.

There was a corral in which I counted more than twenty mounts and before which now stood the horse I had loosed, while its companions nickered a greeting. A man ran from among those busied with the stockade building to catch the reins of the strayed mount. He shouted.

I saw the saffron yellow of a woman's robe in the doorway of the half finished hall, and other colors behind her. The men had downed tools, were gathering around the horse. Old Race all of them, with here and there a lighter head which could mark one of Half-Sulcar strain. And they all wore the leather of fighting men. Whatever this household was now, I was

159

ready to wager all that they had been Borderers not too long ago.

And as a Borderer I could well believe that, as peaceful and open as the scene below appeared from my perch, they had their sentinels and safeguards. So that to win down into their midst would tax any scout's ability. Yet to be found skulking here would do me no good.

The same intricate device as was set on the saddle horn had been freshly painted on the wall of the hall, but I did not recognize it. The only conclusion I dared draw was that the very presence of such a to-be-permanent holding here meant that the dwellers therein believed they had nothing to fear from the south, that Karsten had ceased to be an enemy.

Yet they fortified with a stockade, and they were working with a will to get that up before they finished the hall. Was that merely because they had lived in the midst of danger so long that they could not conceive of any house without such protection?

Now what should I do? This household had come into the wilderness by choice. They might be the very kind I sought. Yet I could not be sure.

Below, they continued to inspect the returned horse, almost as if it had materialized out of air before their eyes, going over the saddle searchingly before they took it off. Several of them gathered together, conferring. Then heads turned, to look to the slope on which I lay. I thought that they had not accepted the idea that the mount had returned of its own will.

The saffron robed woman disappeared, came back again. In her arms were mail shirts, while behind her a slighter figure in a rose-red dress brought helms, their chain-mail throat scarves swinging.

As four of the workers armed themselves in practiced speed, a fifth put fingers to mouth and whistled shrilly. He was answered from at least five points, one of them behind and above me to the left! I flattened yet tighter to the ground. Had I already been sighted by that lookout? If so—why had he not already jumped me? If I had not yet been seen, then any move on my part might betray me at once. I was pinned. Perhaps I had made the wrong choice; to go boldly in would be better than to be caught spying.

I got to my feet, keeping my hands up, palms out before me, well away from my weapons belt. Then I began to walk down. They caught sight of me in seconds.

"Keep on, bold hero!" The voice behind me was sharp. "We like well to see open hands on those who come without verge horn warning."

I did not turn my head as I answered. "You have them in your sight now, sentry. There has been no war glove flung between us—"

"That is as it may be, warrior. Yet friend does not belly-creep upon friend after the manner of one come to collect a head and so enslave the ghost of the slain."

Head-collecting! Refuge holding right enough—not only that, but at least this sentry was one of the fanatics who had made a name for themselves, even in the tough Borderer companies, for the utter ferocity of their fighting. There were those come out of Karsten who had suffered so grievously that they had retreated into barbarian customs to allay, if anything ever could, their well-deep hatred.

I made no haste down that slope and to the holding. The man or men who had chosen to plant it here had an eye for the country. And, once the stockade was complete, they would be very snug against attack. They waited for me in the now gateless opening of that stockade, armed, helmed, though they had not yet drawn sword or gun.

The centermost wore insignia on the fore of his helm, set there in small yellow gem stones. He was a man of middle years, I believed, though with all of us of the Old Race the matter of age is hard to determine, for our life spans are long unless put to an end by violence, and the marks of age do not show until close to the end of that tale of years.

I halted some paces from him. My helm veil was thrown well back, giving him clear view of my features.

"To the House greeting, to those of the House good fortune,

to the day a good dawn and sunset, to the endeavor good fortune without break." I gave the old formal greeting, then waited upon his answer, on which depended whether I could reckon myself tolerated, if not a guest, or find myself a prisoner.

There was something of the same searching measurement as Ethutur had used on me back in the Green Valley. A sword scar had left a white seam long his jaw line, and his mail, though well kept, had been mended on the shoulder with a patch of slightly larger links.

The silence lengthened. I heard a small scuffing behind me and guessed that the guard who had accompanied me was ready to spring at the Manor Lord's order. It was hard not to stand ready to my own defense, to hold my hands high and wait upon another's whim.

"The House of Dhulmat opens its gates to whom?"

I heard a choked sound, a bitten off protest from my guard. Again I was presented with a dilema. To answer with my true name and family clan might condemn me if I had been outlawed, and I had no reason to believe that that had not been done. Yet if this holding already had its gate-crier in place, that protection device would detect a false name instantly as I passed it. I could retreat only to a very old custom, one which had been in abeyance in time of war. Whether it would have any force in the here and now I did not know.

"The House of Dhulmat, on which be the sun, the wind, and the good of wide harvest, opens gates to a geas ordered man." It was the truth and in the far past it meant that I was under certain bounds of speech which none might question without bringing me into peril. I waited once more for the Lord to accept or deny me.

"Gates open to one swearing no threat against Dhulmat, man or clan, roof-tree, field, flock, herd, mount—" He intoned the words slowly as if he pulled them one by one from long buried memory.

I relaxed. That oath could I give without any reservations. He held out his sword blade point to me, a sign I accepted the death it promised were I foresworn. I went to one knee and laid my lips to the cold metal.

"No threat from me to man or clan, roof-tree, field, flock, herd or mount of the House of Dhulmat!"

He must have given some signal I did not detect, for the woman in saffron approached, bearing with both hands a goblet filled with a mixture of water, wine, milk, the true guesting cup. So I knew that here they clung to the old ways, perhaps the more because they had been rift from all which had once been home to them.

My host touched his lips to the edge of the goblet and handed it to me. I swallowed a mouthful and then dribbled a few drops to right and left, to the house and the land, before I passed it back, to go from hand to hand in that company, finally to the guard who now stepped up to my side, shooting me a still suspicious glance. He was a lean mountain wolf right enough, tough and hard as the steel he wore. I knew his like well.

Thus I came into the Manor of Dhulmat—or what was the germ of that manor-to-be. My host was the Lord Hervon, and, though he never said it, I could guess that he must once have been lord of a far larger land than this. The Lady Chriswitha who now headed his household was his second wife—for his first family had vanished during the horning in Karsten. But she had given him two daughters and a son, and both daughters had married landless men who had chosen to join the clan. These, with such shield men as had attached themselves to Hervon during the twenty years or more of border warfare, and the wives of such, had come here to found a new life.

"We marked this valley during patrol," Hervon told me as they put food before me, "and camped here many times during the years, raising part of this hall. You may not understand at your age, but a man needs a place to return to, and this was ours. So when the sealing of the mountains was done and we need no longer bear swords south, then we were minded to set our hearthstone here."

How much dared I ask him concerning what had happened in Estcarp during the time I had been east of the mountains? Yet I had to know.

"Karsten is truly sealed?" I risked that much.

There was a grunt from the other man at the board—Godgar, who had played sentinel in the heights.

Hervon smiled thinly. "So it would seem. We have not yet any real news, but if any of Pagar's force survived that sealing, then he is not a human man. With their army gone and all passes closed, it will be long before they can move again. The Falconers still ride the mountains—where they may find passage, that is—and the eyes of their scout-hawks are ready to report any movements from that filth."

"But Alizon is not sealed," I ventured again.

This time Godgar gave a grating laugh. "Alizon? Those hounds have slunk back to their kennels in a hurry. They do not want to sniff the same kind of storm in *their* noses! For once the Power has been a—"

I saw Hervon shoot him a warning look and he was suddenly silent, flushing a little.

"Yes, the Power has wrought well," I interposed. "Thanks to the Wise Ones we have now a breathing spell."

"The Wise Ones." The Lady Chriswitha seated herself on the bench beside her lord. "But in such action they served themselves ill. The tidings are that they wrung the forces out of them, to their great hurt—many died and others are spent. If Alizon knew of this, surely they would not be so wary of us."

Hervon nodded. "Yes, so you do well, young man, to call this peace a breathing spell." His gaze dropped to the board before him, "Perhaps we waste our strength and our hopes in what we strive to do here now. It is very hard to lose all—"

His lady's hand fell over his in a warming clasp. Then her eyes went to the daughters at the other end of the hall, and those with them. And I was shaken, for, if by some miracle I could rouse such men as these to follow me to the east, what could I offer them save danger once more? Perhaps worse danger than these had fled when they came out of Karsten. Leave them be in their small, hard won time of peace. My memory of the golden land when it was free faded. Though nothing would lift from me the geas in this matter.

Godgar cleared his throat. "You, young man, where do you ride—or walk, since, though you wear horseman's boots, you come hither on your own two feet?"

And the compulsion which had brought me over the mountains set on me now an order for truth though I did not wish to speak in this place where peace was a birth of hope.

"I hunt men—"

"Men—not a man?" Hervon's eyebrows lifted. I thought he had credited me with some motive from his own past, the desire for private vengeance. For a feud vow, taken in the right time and place—or the wrong, depending upon how you looked on the matter—could also be a geas.

"Men—those willing to carve out a new future—" How could I put my mission into words without revealing too much to those inclined to betray me?

Godgar frowned. "You are no Sulcar recruiter for a raiding voyage. To venture this far inland when you could have men beyond counting along the river or in any port would be folly. And if it is a foray against Alizon—the Seneshal has forbidden such, save under his own banner."

"No. I have fighting to offer, but not at sea nor in the north. I offer land—good land—to be sword bought. Where a son may uncover his father's fire to a higher blazing—"

The Lady Chriswitha had been watching me closely. Now she leaned forward a little, holding me with her gaze as if she were one of the Witches, able to pick true from false in my very brain.

"And where lies this land of yours, stranger?"

I wet my lips with tongue tip. This was the time of testing. "To the east," I said.

They were all blank of countenance. Did the block hold so tight that no thought of Escore could ever penetrate, that I could *not* arouse any of them even to think of such a journey?

"East?" She repeated that with complete incomprehension, as if I had used a word entirely without meaning. "East?" she said again, and this time it was a sharp-asked question.

This was a gamble, but all my life had been a wagering of one risk against another. I must learn here and now what luck I would have with any men such as these. Tell them the truth as we had discovered it, see if that truth would free them from the bonds tied long ago.

So I spoke of what Kemoc had discovered at Lormt, and of what we had found over the mountains sealed in that long ago. Yet in that telling I did not reveal my own identity, and it was that fact the Lady Criswitha struck upon unerringly when I had done.

"If all this be so—then how is it that you went over these mountains you say we cannot remember, or are not allowed to remember, and which have been so long closed to us? Why did not such bonds hold you also?" Her suspicion was plain.

But her lord, as if he had not heard her, spoke now:

"This much is true, I have never thought of the east. In Karsten, yes, but here—no. It was as if that direction did not exist."

"The Lady has asked a question which needs an answer," growled Godgar from the other side. "I would like to hear it, too."

There could be no more disguise. To prove my truth I must tell all—the reason for my going estward. And I put it directly.

"For two reasons did I go. I am outlawed, or believe that I am, and I am not fully of your blood."

"I knew it!" Godgar's fist raised menacingly, though he did not strike with it. "Outlawed, yet he tricked you into guesting him, Lord. And with such a guest bond does not hold. Cut him down, else he bring us new troubles!"

"Hold!" Hervon cut through that hot speech. "What name do you bear, outlaw? And talk of geas will not cover you now."

"I am Kyllan of the House of Tregarth."

For a second or two I thought that they did not know, that

that name meant nothing here. Then Godgar roared in wrath and this time his fist sent me sprawling, my head ringing. I had no chance in my defense, for his men were in the hall and they piled on me before I could even gain my knees. Another blow sent me into darkness and I awoke, with an aching head and bruised body, to yet more darkness.

From very faint traces of light outlining a door—or at least an entrance—well above me and the feel of pounded, hardened earth under my body, my hands being locked in rope loops, I concluded that I now lay in a storage place which must antedate, maybe by several years, this half completed manor. I had helped to construct just such supply pits in the past, deep dug in the earth, floored and walled with stone if possible, if not with hardened clay, to be covered by a trap door.

Why did I still live? By rights they could have taken my life there in the hall. Apparently Godgar, at least, knew me for what I had been undoubtedly proclaimed. That they had not killed me at once probably meant they planned to deliver me to the authorities of the Council, and perhaps the first ending was the one I should desire the most.

As a recruiter I was a failure indeed. One can always see one's mistakes afterwards, as plain as the victors' shields hung on the outwalls of a conquered keep. But I had never claimed to be clever at such work. How long would I lie here? I believed this holding to be one far to the southeast, perhaps the only one now in this section of the country. Any messenger to the authorities might have more than a day's travel, even if he took extra mounts for relays. Unless, of course, there was an adept trained in sending somewhere in the neighborhood.

I squirmed around, though the movement added to the pain in my head, and I had to fight nausea. Whoever had tied that confining rope knew his business well. I stopped my fruitless struggling, since no energy of mine was going to free me. To free me—had I the slightest hope left?

But if I was going to be given up to the Council, there was something I must do, if I could, for others. Would the

Witches ever dare to turn east? They might. Who can foretell any action when he has not even the dimmest of foresight? Those on the other side of the mountain must be warned.

Matter would not aid me—but mind? I concentrated, building my mental picture of Kaththea, straining to contact my sister wherever she might be. Faint—very faint—a stirring. But no more than that shadow of a shadow. Kemoc? Having tried the greater first, now I strove for the lesser. And this time received not even a shadow reply.

So much for our talent. Dahaun had been wrong when she had suggested I might communicate so in extremity. Dahaun? I set her in my mind as I had seen her last.

Shadow—deeper than shadow—not real contact as I had with brother and sister so that words and messages might pass from mind to mind, but enough to give warning. Instantly there was a beating at me in return—only it was as if someone shouted to me in a foreign tongue some frantic message which I could not understand. I lay gasping under the pressure of that unintelligible sending. It snapped, and was gone.

My breath came in fast, shallow gasps; my heart pounded as if I raced before some enemy host. There was a sound, but it was of this world and not from that place outside. The crack of light about the opening above grew larger and a ladder thudded down. They were coming for me. I braced myself for action which I must face.

A whisper of robes. I tried to hold my head higher. Why had the Lady Chriswitha come alone? The door fell behind her so that the gloom was again complete as she came to stand over me. I caught the scent of that sweet fern women use to lay between fresh washed garments.

She was stooping very close above me. "Tell me why you fled Estcarp."

There was urgency in her demand, but the why of it I did not understand. What made the reason of our escape of any importance now?

I told her the whole of it, making a terse statement of facts and fears as we three had known them. She listened without interruption, then:

168

"The rest of it. The lost land—the chance to bring it once more under our rule—?"

"Under the rule of good instead of evil, through a war," I corrected. Again I was puzzled, and asked:

"What matters all this to you, lady?"

"Perhaps nothing, or perhaps much. They have sent a messenger to the nearest ward keep, and it will go then by sending to Es Castle. Afterward—they will come for you."

"I had expected no less." I was glad my voice held steady when I said that.

Her robes swished. I knew she was turning away from me. But from the foot of the ladder she spoke once more:

"Not all minds are the same in some matters. Outlaws have been born because of laws not all hold by."

"What do you mean?"

She gave me no straight reply, only saying, "Good fortune go with you, Kyllan of Tregarth. You have given me much to think on."

I heard her climb the ladder, saw her raise the door. Then she was gone, leaving me in turn with things to think on—though to no profitable purpose.

XVII

THEY CAME for me at last, on a morning when there were clouds across the sky and the softness of coming rain in the air. There were Godgar and three others, but, to my surprise, no Council guard. I do not know how long I had lain in the

169

store-pit. They had brought me food and drink, but those who came so singly would answer no questions. I had time for many thoughts, but there were no more dreams. Except those I wove deliberately when awake, riding the golden land with one—but there is no need to dwell upon those.

Now they produced a mount for me—a sorry animal, probably the worst of their stable—and they lashed me into the saddle as if they thought that I might suddenly produce the claws and fangs of a wolf-man. Save for these four there was no sign of life about the manor. That I wondered about . . . until my wonder became a tremor of uneasiness. It almost seemed that this expedition could be of Godgar's planning alone, and there had been nothing in his attitude since our first meeting to suggest that he designed any good end for me.

He took the fore in our ride out, my mount led by the rider just behind, the other two bringing up the rear. They were all older men, those guards, enough like their leader to have been fashioned in one dart stamper. And, while they did not use me with any unnecessary roughness, yet neither did I see any hope of escape.

We turned north as we came out on the manor road, which was no more than a track of beaten earth. The pace Godgar set was that of any routine patrol, not forced, yet designed to eat miles. I glanced over my shoulder at the manor. The matter of the Lady Chriswitha's visit still puzzled me. I had not dared to believe that anything in my favor might come of it. But still I thought that it had shown minds divided on some subjects within those half completed walls. But the manor might now be deserted.

None of the guards spoke, nor did I see any reason to ask questions. We merely rode, first under clouds, and then in the beginning of a drizzle which seemed to effect them no more than might the sun of a pleasant day.

In spite of the hopelessness of my situation I continued to study those who accompanied me, and the land about, trying to sight any chance for a break. My hands were bound before me to the high horn of my saddle, my feet lashed to the stirrups, the reins of my horse in the hands of him who rode before me. My helm was gone, though they had left me my mail shirt. There were no weapons in my belt. And the horse under me could be easily run down by any they bestrode.

As for the country, we were in open land where there was little or no cover. The grass, which brushed as high as our stirrups beyond the edge of the narrow road, was autumn yellowed. And the rain was chill. But there were inhabitants in that grass. I saw prong-horns race away, their great startleaps carrying them well into the air. And birds flew—

I do not know why I began to watch the sky for any hint of green wings. It might be more probable for a Flannan to perch suddenly on the saddle horn above my tied hands. Yet each time I saw a bird I looked the closer.

Then Godgar reined up, waiting for my leader to catch level with him. He said something in a low voice and the rein passed from guard to commander, the relieved man spurring ahead, Godgar pulling at the reins until my horse was beside his. He had fastened his helm veil across his throat and chin as if we were about to go into battle, and over that half mask of tiny metallic links his eyes were hot.

"Who sent you, oath breaker? Who sent you to bring down the House of Dhulmat?"

His demand made no sense to me.

"I am neither oath-breaker, nor one who wishes ill to you and yours."

Tied as I was I could not escape the answering blow which made my head ring and swayed me in the saddle.

"We know ways to make a man talk," he snarled. "Karsten taught us much!"

"Perhaps you can make a man talk," I got out, "but this man does not know what you seek."

Luckily, though he had come to depend upon pain and force to support his orders, he had a measure of intelligence behind such brutality. Now he chose to use it.

"You go to the Council. If you are who you say, you know what they will do to you."

171

"Assuredly." To Godgar the warrior's creed was a living thing and part of that was a fatalistic acceptance of things as they were. I could do no more than summon that to my aid now.

"They will wring out of you all knowledge; thus we shall learn sooner or later what we want to know. Why not tell us now—who sent you to take refuge with Hervon and so blacken his name?"

"No one. I came by chance to—"

"Riding one of our horses, a mount that bolted without warning from our holding and returned two days later only a little before you? By your own telling, oath-breaker, you have consorted with witchery, so all could be of your doing. But the why of it? Why do you move against Hervon? We have no family-feud with you! Who told you to do this?"

"Any holding would have suited me," I said wearily. There was no way of making him believe that. He was determined that I meant ill to his lord. But that private feuds were still alive among the Old Race refugees was new to me. Apparently Godgar expected such now. "A geas was laid upon me in Escore, even as I told you. I was to recruit such of the Old Race as wanted to try to free the land from which they once sprang."

I half expected a second blow, a demand that I speak what he would consider the truth. But to my surprise, Godgar turned his head with deliberation and looked to the east. Then he laughed, a harsh bark.

"Did you think such a story would win you a fighting tail into nowhere, outlaw? Why, I could think of two handsful of words which would serve you better in Hervon's listening!"

"Have it your own way then," I told him, tired of argument. "This is the bare bones of it. My sister was forced to enter the Place of Wisdom against her will. She shared with me and my brother a gift. Through that she reached Kemoc before the time of her final Vow, for she would not be one of the Witches. We had her forth from the Place, since the safeguards of the Power were exhausted by the closing of the mountains. Having won her freedom we strove to preserve it by striking east, into the unknown. We crossed the forbidden passes, found Escore, and those there, both enemy and friend, with the need for men to fight on the side of good in a very old war. Through no wish of mine—that I shall swear to by any Sign or Name—it was laid upon me to come here, and to seek out any willing to cross the mountains. More than that no wile nor force can learn from me, for that is the full truth!"

He no longer laughed; instead his eyes regarded me very narrowly over the veil of his helm.

"I have heard of the Warder of the South, of Simon Tregarth—"

"And of the Lady Jaelithe," I added for him. "And never has it been hidden that he was an outlander and held some of the Power—is that not so?"

He nodded reluctantly.

"Then can it also be beyond the bounds of belief that we, the flesh of their flesh, have also gifts not usual to others? We were born, at one birth, and always have we been locked of spirit, and sometimes of mind. When Kaththea wanted to come forth from that Place, we could no nothing else than bring her. If that makes us meat for any man's sword, then that is the way matters stand."

This time Godgar made me no answer, but set his horse on, pulling sharply at the leading reins. We trotted down the rough road in a thick drizzle. Nor did he speak with me again throughout that long morning. We made a noonday stop in a place of rocks where an overhanging ledge gave shelter and there was a supply of wood laid up by a blackened ring of stones to mark a known camping place.

I walked stiffly when they had me down from my horse, for they left my legs free but not my hands. They produced journey bread, dried meat and fruit, little better than field rations. And they loosed my hands to eat, though one of them stood over me until I was done, then promptly applied the lashings again. But to my surprise they did not mount up after they had eaten. Instead one of them set a fire, which we had not needed for the cooking of food, taking what seemed to me unnecessary care in just how the wood was placed. Then, when light was put to that stack of wood, he took a stand to the right of it, a cloak in his hands.

Signaling! Though the code they used was none I knew from my scouting days. Blink, blink, blink, back and forth he snapped the cloak. I stared out on the gloomy countryside, straining to read anywhere along the darkened horizon an answer to those flashes. But without result.

However, my guards seemed satisfied. They kept the fire going, after letting it die down a little, sitting about it while their cloaks and surcoats steamed dry. I watched the sodden countryside. They were waiting—for whom and why?

Godgar cleared his throat, and the sound was loud in that place, for they had not spoken more than a few words since they had dismounted.

"We wait for those who will take you to deliver to the Council guards," he addressed me. "There will be no one then who can say that you sheltered with Hervon."

"As you youself said, when they question me under the Power, the Wise Ones will know all." I could not understand why he tried this clumsy coverup of passing me from one party to another.

"Perhaps."

Then it came to me: there was one way in which I could not be so questioned, and that was if I was delivered dead! If my body was so brought in by a middle party, there could be no connection then with Hervon's people.

"Why leave the throat cutting to another?" I asked then. "You have a sword to your hand."

When he did not reply I continued: "Or do you wear a rune sword which will flame out with blood on it—to be read thereafter by all men? Your lord was not one with you in this. He would not set point or edge to a man with tied wrists!"

Godgar stirred. His eyes were hot again; I had pricked him then. Hard as he was, old customs still held. And there flashed now into my mind, as if some voice spoke the words into my ears, an oath considered so potent and binding that no man who had ever borne a sword in war could break it.

"You know me—I am Kyllan of Tregarth. I have ridden with the Border Scouts—is that not fact? Have you heard any ill report of such riding?"

He might not understand the why of my asking, but he returned frankly enough:

"I have heard of you with the Scouts. You were a warrior— and a man—in those days."

"Then listen well, Godgar and you others—" I paused, and then spoke each word that followed with emphasis and measured slowness, as my sister might have delivered one of her chants to summon the Power.

"May I be slain by my own blade, struck by my own darts, if I ever meant any ill to those within the House of Dhulmat, or to any man of Estcarp."

They stared at me across their veils. I had given them the strongest assurance any of our calling might ever use. Would it hold?

They stirred uneasily, and their eyes went from me to each other. Godgar tugged at his helm veil, bringing it in a loose loop from his jaw as if he were about to eat once more.

"That was ill done!" he barked angrily.

"Ill done?" I shot back. "In what way, Godgar? I have given you Sword Oath that I mean you and yours no ill. What evil lies in that?"

Then I turned to his men. "Do you believe me?"

They hesitated, then he in the center spoke. "We believe because we must."

"Then where lies the ill doing?"

Godgar got to his feet and strode back and forth a few paces, his frown blackly heavy. He stopped and rounded on me.

"We have begun a thing for the sake of those to whom we owe allegiance. You are no one, nothing. Why must your fate be made now a shadow on our shield honor? What witchery have you used, outlaw?"

175

"No witchery, save that which you, and you,"—I pointed to each—"and you, and you, Godgar, share with me. I am warrior bred; I did what I had to do in the support of my own allegiances. That put me outside the law of the Council. I came back here because I was laid under another command— the why of it and by whom I have no knowing. But that I meant ill by my coming no Power can prove, for it is not so."

"Too late." Another of the guards was standing, pointing into the open.

Dim as the clouds made the scene, the coming riders could be counted. Five . . . six of them.

Godgar nodded in their direction. "Those owe us a battle debt. But since you say you came to Hervon by chance, and have taken oath on it—well, they will turn you in living, not dead. With the Witches you can take your chances and those will not be bright. I—I am not honor broke in this, outlaw!"

"You are not honor broke," I agreed.

"Wait!"

He who had indicated the riders now spoke more sharply. "What is—what is that?"

Between the distant riders and our shelter there was open country, covered only with the tall grass. It was at that grass he pointed now. It rippled, was like the sea with each wave troubled and wind tossed. And through it came such a regiment as no man among us had ever seen. Prong-horns, not leaping away in alarm, but gathering with purpose towards us. A shambling bear taking no notice, a grass cat—yellow-brown, but equal to his brothers of the snow lines—smaller things we could not distinguish save for the movement in the grass . . . all headed to us!

"What will they do?" Godgar was disconcerted as he would never have been to see an armed party about to attack. The very unnaturalness of this advance was unnerving.

I struggled to my feet and none reached a hand to stay me, for they were too awed by what they now witnessed.

As the grass was agitated by a gathering of four-footed inhabitants, so was the sky filled in turn. Birds came in flocks out of nowhere, and they swooped, called, strove to reach us under the ledge. These men had endured years of war such as only warrior blood could face, but this was against nature.

I struggled to contact the minds of those closing in upon us. I found that I could contact them, yes, and read their determination—but I could not control them in any manner.

I moved away from the others, who had drawn tightly under the protection of the ledge. The birds whirred, screamed, trilled about me, but they made no move to attack. Grass dwellers gathered about my feet, and wove circles, always facing—not me—but those who had brought me here. I began to walk, out into the open and the rain, away from Godgar and his men.

"Stand—or I shoot!"

I glanced back. His dart gun was out, aimed at me. Through the air came that which I had sought—blue-green, moving swiftly, straight for Godgar's head. He cried out, and ducked. I walked on, passing a grass cat growling deep in its throat and lashing its tail, looking not to me but to the men behind, past a prong-horn that snorted, struck the earth with blade-sharp hooves, past a gathering army in fur and feathers.

And always I probed, trying to find the will which had launched that army, which held them there. For that such existed I was certain. The horses that had carried us snorted, screamed, reared to break loose from their picket ropes and run, in wild galloping, from feline forms skulking about. I heard shouts behind me, but this time I did not turn to look. If I were to die by Godgar's darts, why face them? Better to walk towards freedom.

I discovered that walking with tied hands was not walking free. The rain had made the ground slippery, and I lost balance with my arms so tightly confined. I had to watch my footing as I went. Then I heard sounds from behind strange enough to make me look.

Just as I had walked away from the ledge, so after me stumbled and wavered my captors—not willingly, but under complusion. For they were being herded by the animals and birds. What had become of their weapons I did not know, but their dart guns were gone. And, strangely enough, none had drawn steel. So they came, strained of face, staring of eye, men caught up in a nightmare of mad dreaming.

I had headed east, and so east we went in company, the birds always above, and always around us the host of animals large and small. Now they gave voice, squeaks, growls, snorts, almost as if they protested their use in this fashion—for being used they were. I glanced to where we had seen those other riders. There was no sign of them! Could they have been overwhelmed by the weird army?

Of all the marches I had made in a lifetime, that was the strangest. The creatures kept pace with me, and those after me, to the best of their ability. Though, after a space, the smaller ones fell behind, and only the larger beasts matched us. The birds went in flocks, wheeling and diving. But the blue-green one had once more vanished.

We plodded on, to what goal I had no idea, though not to return to Hervon's holding. Again and again I tried to reach by contact the control over that furred and feathered force. Finally in my mind the old march cadence began its well-known sing-song:

"Sky-earth-mountain-stone! Sword cuts to the bone!" Then I realized I was chanting that aloud and the clamor of beast and bird was stilled. Yet silent they marched with a determination not of their natures.

At length I paused and turned to face those behind me. They were pale under the brown weathering on their faces. And they met my gaze glassily, as men will front something over which they have no domination, against which they can make no true stand.

"Godgar!" I raised my voice sharply to shake him out of that ensorcellment. "Godgar, go from here by your path, as long as it leads back to the House of Dhulmat. As I have said, between us lies no feud, nor the need for any answer to be made to this day's work. If I wore a sword I would exchange it now for your blade in truce."

He had passed beyond anger, but he was not broken.

"Captain"—that address of respect came wryly from him—"if it is peace you offer, peace shall we take. But do those who walk with us also offer it?"

That I did not know either, but it must be tested. "Try them," I replied.

Then, watching warily their flankers, Godgar and his men started south. Slowly, with a semblance of reluctance, a way was opened to them. As he saw this, Godgar's shoulders went back a fraction more. He looked once more to me.

"This must be reported," he said.

"Let it be so," I answered.

"Wait!" He started towards me. A grass cat crouched, fangs bared, snarling. Godgar stopped short. "I mean you no ill. Walking with bound hands is hard; I would free you."

But the cat would have none of that, despite my silent command.

"It would seem that *our* oaths are not current coin here, Godgar. Go you in peace, and report as you must. And I say again—I hold no feud thought against you or yours."

He returned to his men and they walked south, behind them trailing a detachment of the creatures, as if they were to be escorted on their way. But for me there was another path—blue-green wings again in the air and a trill of song urging me along it.

XVIII

IT WAS a little later that I learned I was not being escorted, but after a manner herded also. For once Godgar and his men were out of sight, I paused, faced about—and looked into the snarling mask of a grass cat, behind it a prong-horn snorting and pawing earth. Ancient enemies, but now united in purpose. The cat growled; I wheeled to face east and the growling ceased. More and more of the furred company had fallen away from the body which had set us moving away from the ledge, but I still led a formidable force, mostly of larger creatures.

A trilling overhead—Dahaun's messenger circled there, urging me on, I thought. So I left the road, tramped on in the sodden grass which brushed wetly about me almost thigh high and sometimes concealed my escort altogether. When I was on the move once more, the bird flashed ahead.

Dahaun—had she followed across the mountains? But sense was against that. There was so close a tie between her race and Escore that they could not go out of that haunted land. Kemoc? But the command over this company of beasts and birds was not Kemoc's, nor Kaththea's, nor born of any magic ever brewed in Estcarp.

Ahead was the dark mass of broken mountains. This route would bring me into their foothills. I struggled against the cords about my wrists. Once into that rough country I would need use of my hands. The ties cut into my flesh and I felt the slipperiness of blood oozing from ridged cuts.

Perhaps that loosened them sufficiently at last. For, in spite of menacing growls and snorts, I halted now and again to work with all my might at those circlets. Then, with a tearing of skin, I pulled one hand free and brought both before me, congested and purple, blood-stained. I wriggled fingers to restore circulation.

The rain had ceased but there was no lightening of the clouds, now that it was twilight. Not only the coming of dark in this wilderness plagued me, but fatigue had slowed my progress to a weary shuffle. I glanced behind. The head of a prong-horn buck was up, the eyes of a cat watched—but farther back. I took a step or so in their direction. Snarl and snort—warning me on. I could see other bodies crouched or erect in the grass. There was for me no road to the west.

They did not follow me, merely stood where they were now, a barrier before those lands where I might find others of my kind. Just as those hunters had been on my trail before, so now these were harrying me out of Estcarp.

Seeing a rocky outcrop not too far away, I made for that and sat down to rest aching feet. Riding boots had never been fashioned for steady hours of walking. I could spy those sentinels slipping along the ground if they were felines, treading on determined hooves for prong-horns. The heavily built bears had disappeared, perhaps unable to keep up. But for the others . . . we matched stares while I thought.

It would seem that someone or something wished to send me back to Escore. And I rebelled against such pressure. First send me to Estcarp on a fruitless mission, then drive me out again. I could see no sense in this, nor does any man take easily to the knowledge that he is only a piece on some game-board, to be moved hither and thither for purposes which are none of his.

Dermont had told me once of a very ancient custom of Karsten, one which had fallen into disuse when the Old Race lost rule there and the newcomers from still farther south had overrun the land. But in dim history there had been a game played each decade. Carven pieces were set out on a marked board. At one side sat him who was deemed the greatest

181

lord, on the other one who was landless, followerless, the least, but who would dare the game. And the landless player represented the forces of disruption and ill luck, while the lord those of confidence and success. Thus they played, not only for all the great lord held, but also for the luck and fortune of the whole land. For, should the landless topple the lord, a period of chaos and change would ensue in the land.

Was such a game now in progress, with a living man—me—for one of its pieces? In Estcarp abode the settled state of things as they are, well established, even firmer now that Karsten had been dealt with. And uneasy Escore where old troubles stirred was the opposite. Perhaps behind that ancient game had lain some older truth well buried, that a more powerful action once known had been reduced to ritual at a gameboard.

So could I speculate, but I doubted that I would ever know how much of my guessing was the truth. I had certainly been moved into Estcarp, just as I was being moved out again. I shook my head, though only the beasts saw that gesture. Then I began to pull up the grass about my rock, making a nest bed. The one thing I *was* sure of was that I could go no farther now.

Though I lay in the open this was one night I felt no need for watch keeping. Perhaps I had been lifted out of the normal courses to the point where I no longer cared, or perhaps I was too tired and worn by what had chanced.

Thus I slept. And if I dreamed, I did not carry the memory of those dreams past my waking. But when I got stiffly to my feet from that mass of grass in the morning, I faced the mountains. This was right—if I were a piece on a gameboard, then I had been moved. I started off with empty hands, no food, and a hard climb before me. Twice I looked back. If my herders had kept vigil during the night that had not lasted until this hour. No sign of them was visible. Neither was there in me any need to go out once more into Estcarp.

During the day I was certainly one under some order, though I could not have put it into words. The broken mountains were my goal. Senseless, senseless, one part of my mind repeated over and over. Urge me in, bring me out—what had I accomplished? A meeting with refugees on a single holding, and on them I have made only a negative impression.

I thought I had been sent to recruit—but my feeble effort had not even begun that task. So—and that brought me up short as I halted on the verge of a mountain reaching ravine—so what *had* been the real reason for my return to Estcarp? I kicked viciously at a stone, sent it rolling from me with a sound to break the general silence.

A use for me—what? None that I could see, and my ignorance gnawed, plunging me into action, the only kind open to me now, the return over-mountain. I scrambled down slope, began to run almost blindly, taking little heed of my body with my mind so bedeviled with frightening half-thoughts to which there were no sane answers.

A fall was the end of that witless race, witless because there was no escaping from fears I bore with me. I lay panting on the earth, beating my still swollen hands on the gravel until the pain of that contact shocked me back to quiet again.

Once the blood stopped pounding so heavily in my ears I heard the gurgle of water and I was drawn by that, my dry mouth gaping even before I reached a spring fed pool. I lapped up the fresh liquid as might one of the hunting cats. Water cold against my face restored more rational thinking. To run terror stricken was never an answer, so—yield to this mysterious ordering until more could be learned. I was far more a man when I left the spring. There was an explanation somewhere and it could only lie in Escore. For the beast army was not of Estcarp's devising. So the sooner I gained to Escore, that much earlier would I learn my place in the new scheme of things.

Hunger grew in me. It had been a long time since I had chewed those trail rations under the rock ledge. Yet nowhere in this wilderness was there food. But I had known hunger before and kept on the move in spite of its twinges. The mountains—could I find again that valley which led to our climb point? Sometimes when I looked about me, either that peculiar distortion which had plagued us before was in force,

183

or else my lack of food worked upon my vision, for there was a disorientation to this land through which I moved.

Evening did not stop me, for the need of Escore had grown to an all pervading urge. I stumbled on, in a narrow cut, but whether the right one I could not have said. And then— ahead was light! Stupidly I plowed to a halt and blinked. I had a dull fear that I had been forestalled, that I was awaited now by those who would cut me off, take me once more captive.

My mind worked so sluggishly that I could see no way out of such disaster. If I retreated it could only be back to the plains, or to be lost in the foothills where I could never find my way again.

Brother!

So deep was I sunk in my own inner pit that at first that mind call meant nothing. Then—then— Kemoc!

I do not believe that I shouted that name aloud as I began to run towards the fire—but in me was a welling fountain of recognition.

He came to meet me and I could not have made those last steps, few as they were, alone. Half guiding, half supporting, he brought me to his oasis of light and warmth. I leaned against a backing of springy brush and held a small bowl, the warmth of its contents reaching my hands, the aroma making me eager to sip at a thick stew.

Kemoc—wearing the garb of Dahaun's people—even to the whip stock at his belt, yet looking as he had a hundred times before when we had shared patrol camps. And the familiarity of the scene was as soothing to my feeling of being under another's control, as the stew was to my hunger of body.

"You knew I was coming?" I broke the silence first, for he had allowed me those moments in which to soak up ease and reassurance.

"She did—The Lady of Green Silence." He sounded a little restrained and aloof. "She told us you were taken—"

"Yes."

"They would not let Kaththea try to aid you. They put a

184

mind lock on her!" Now his constraint was hostile. "But they could not hold me. So having wrought their own magic, they allowed me to come to see how well it worked."

A small flash of insight—did Kemoc, also, feel that he was now moved by another's will?

"*Their* magic." The beasts—yes, that could well be Dahaun's magic.

"They were not sure it would work—not in Estcarp. But it seems that it did, since you are here. Kyllan, why did you go?" he demanded of me hotly.

"Because I had to." And I told him of what and how it had chanced with me since my awaking from that dream in the Green Valley. Nor did I hide from him my concern over being used by some unknown authority for a reason I did not understand.

"Dahaun?" Again that sharpness.

I shook my head. "No, she did not wish it. But I tell you, Kemoc, in all of this we play a game, and it is not of our choosing or understanding. Least of all do I know why I was sent here and then allowed—no, ordered—to return again!"

"They say there is an ingathering of forces in Escore, a rallying of evil—and they move to summon their people also. The time of truce is past; both move now to a trial of strength. And I tell you, brother, hard as this may be, still I welcome it. For I do not relish this play behind a screen."

"Kaththea—you say they have mind locked her."

"Only until she would agree not to use her Power. They said it would only further awaken all we have to fear. She waits with the others, up there." He gestured at the mountain wall behind him. "With the day we shall join them."

This night I did not sleep dreamlessly. Once more I rode the fields of Escore in another guise—mailed, armed, ready for bared swords or worse. And with me was a force of those to choose to share shields. Among them were faces I knew from the past, but not all from a distant past. For, mailed and armed as was the custom in times of great danger, I saw the Lady Criswitha. Once she smiled at me before she rode on and others of the Old Race took her place. But always we

185

traveled with danger to the right and left, and a kind of desperation eating at us. There was a banner fashioned like a huge green bird (or could it have been a real bird many times life size?) and the wind appeared to whip it so the wings were ever spread in flight. Always we bore with us an axe's weight of death, not tribute, to satisfy any dark overlord.

"Kyllan!" I awoke with Kemoc's hand on my shoulder, shaking me into consciousness.

"You had ill dreams," he told me.

"Perhaps ill, perhaps otherwise. You shall have your open battles, Kemoc, one after another of them. Whether we shall cleanse the land or be buried in it—" I shrugged. "At any rate we have our hands, and swords for them to use. Though it may be that time does not favor us."

For the second time we climbed the cliff out of Estcarp. And for all the urgency riding me I moved slowly. But when we had reached the crest, before we moved on to the pass, I turned, as did Kemoc. He had a distance lens to his eyes. Suddenly his body tensed and I knew he had sighted something.

"What is it?"

His answer was to pass the lenses to me. Trees and rocks leaped up at me. Among them men moved. So they were a-hunting on my track again? Well, that would not last; they would shy off from the forbidden lands as had those others. A large force—truly they wanted me badly.

Then I focussed the glasses better and I saw one rider, another, a third. Unbelieving, I looked to Kemoc. He nodded, his surprise open to read on his face.

"You see truly, brother—those are in part women!"

"But—why? Wise Ones come to capure the fugitive for themselves?"

"What Wise One would bear a child in a riding cradle before her?"

I raised the lenses again, swept that company, found what he had earlier marked, a cloaked woman in the breeches meant for long and hard riding, but across her saddle the cradle of a child still too young to sit a pony.

"Some invasion—they being hunted before it—" I sought for the only explanation I could credit.

"I think not. They ride from the southwest. Invasion now would come only from Alizon in the north. No, I believe they are recruits—the recruits you were sent for, brother."

"That cannot be—women and children?" I protested. "And I told my story only at Hervon's manor where it was discredited when I named myself outlaw. There was no reason for them to—"

"No reason that you knew of," he corrected.

I do not know why at that moment I remembered something from my childhood. I had come into the hall at Etsford on one of those rare occasions when my father had visited us. Yes, it was the time that he had brought Otkell to be our tutor in arms. And he was speaking of something which had lately happened at Gorm. A Sulcar ship from overseas had drifted into harbor, all her crew dead on board. And in the Captain's cabin, written out in the log, the story of a plague picked up in a distant port, which spread from man to man. Those at Gorm towed the ship well to sea, set her afire to burn and sink, taking her dead with her. But all had come from one man, returning from shore leave with the seeds of death in him.

Supposing I had been sent to Estcarp carrying some such seed—not directly of disease and death, though the end result might well be the latter, but to infect those about me with the need to seek Escore? Wild as it was that could be an explanation to answer more than one question.

Kemoc read it in my mind and now he took the lenses from me, to once more study those moving with such purpose towards us.

"They do not seem to be befogged, or otherwise blocked," he observed. "Your plague may already be well seated."

Women and children—no! A tail of fighting men, those with no ties who were long hardened by slim chances—that

187

I had wished for. But to bring their families into the threat of shadowed Escore— *No!*

"It would appear that *someone* or *something* has plans for refounding a nation." Kemoc lowered the lenses.

"More players for the game!" I knew dull anger and also that such anger would not avail me. Nor would I take the lenses again as Kemoc held them out. This was my doing and I would have to answer for it.

"They cannot bring their mounts in," Kemoc said, becoming practical. I could almost have struck him for his quick acceptance of what was to come. "But with ropes their gear may be lifted, and they aided. Then, perhaps, horned ones waiting beyond the tree valley—"

"You are very sure they are coming to us," I shot at him.

"Because he is right!"

Kaththea stood behind us. Now she ran forward, her hand on my arm, on Kemoc's, linking us.

"Why?" Somewhere in her, I hoped, was an answer for me.

"Why do they come? Not all of them will, only those able to feel the call, the need. And why were you sent, Kyllan? Because you were the one of us who could best carry the seed of that call. In me the dream could not be set; I had too many Power safeguards implanted. In Kemoc also, for he was so close of mind that my block spread to him. So you had to be the carrier, the sower . . . and now comes the harvest!"

"To their deaths!"

"Some to death," my sister agreed. "But do not all living things abide with death from the first drawing of life breath? No man may order the hour of his dying if he travels by life's pattern. Nor can you bewail the chance, brother, which made you carry your dream into Estcarp. We stand in a time of chance and change, and move into new designs we do not understand. Play your life boldly as you always have. Do you blame the sword for killing? It is the hand and brain behind it which holds the responsibility!"

"And who is the hand and brain behind this?"

"Who can name the names of the Eternal Ones?"

Her prompt reply startled me. That some still believed in those nameless forces beyond nature, man, or the world, I knew. That those of witch training would, I could not understand.

"Yes, Kyllan, the acquiring of learning does not mean the end of faith, even though some who stop too soon would swear that so. I do not know in *whose* pattern we begin to move now, nor do I deny that it may be a harsh one with sore troubles ahead. But we are caught in it and there is no turning back. Meanwhile, cease chewing fingers and become yourself!"

So was the incoming to Escore. And I, who had been challenging death since I first felt the weight of a sword above my hip, took on again that weight and others. For we did thereafter indeed buy Escore with steel, raw courage, and such witchery as was not tainted. And that winning is a marvelous tale which must have a full chronicle to itself. But this was the beginning of that tale, the sowing of the seed from which came later harvest—and it was the story of us three.

The Gregg Press Science Fiction Series

David G. Hartwell, *Editor*

L. W. Currey, *Associate Editor*

The Witch World Novels of Andre Norton is a special publication of The Gregg Press Science Fiction Series, a major publishing program offering library-bound hardcover editions of the best in science fiction. In most cases the Gregg edition is the first hardcover edition published in the United States. For further information about these titles, please inquire at your library or write to Gregg Press at the address given following the list of published titles in the series.

Series I

Alfred Bester, *The Stars My Destination* (1957). With a New Introduction by Paul Williams. 216 pp.

Karel Čapek, *War with the Newts* (1937). With a New Introduction by Darko Suvin. 376 pp.

Charles Romyn Dake, *A Strange Discovery* (1899). With New Introductions by Thomas D. Clareson and L. W. Currey. 336 pp.

Mary Griffith, *Three Hundred Years Hence* (1836). With an Introduction by Nelson F. Adkins and a New Preface by David G. Hartwell. 144 pp.

Edmond Hamilton, *The Horror on the Asteroid and Other Tales of Planetary Horror* (1936). 272 pp.

Will. N. Harben, *The Land of the Changing Sun* (1894). With a New Introduction by L. W. Currey. 256 pp.

Thea von Harbou, *Metropolis* (1929). With a New Introduction by Peter Minichiello and 17 stills from the film version. 264 pp.

Mary Bradley Lane, *Mizora* (1890). With New Introductions by Stuart A. Teitler and Kristine A. Anderson. 160 pp.

Richard Adams Locke, *The Moon Hoax* (1835). With a New Introduction by Ormond Seavey and appendixes. 112 pp.

Jack London, *The Science Fiction of Jack London: An Anthology*, edited with a New Introduction by Richard Gid Powers. 536 pp.

Walter M. Miller, Jr., *A Canticle for Leibowitz* (1959). With a New Introduction by Norman Spinrad. 336 pp.

Mary Shelley, *Tales and Stories of Mary Wollstonecraft Shelley* (1891). With a New Introduction by Joanna Russ. 424 pp.

W. Olaf Stapledon, *To The End of Time* (1953). With a New Introduction by Curtis C. Smith. 808 pp.

Van Tassel Sutphen, *The Doomsman* (1906). With a New Introduction by Thomas D. Clareson. 336 pp.

Chauncey Thomas, *The Crystal Button* (1891). With a New Introduction by Ormond Seavey. 368 pp.

George Tucker ("Joseph Atterley"), *A Voyage to the Moon* (1827). With a New Preface by David G. Hartwell and an appendix. 304 pp.

Jules Verne, *An Antarctic Mystery* (1899). With a New Introduction by David G. Hartwell. 360 pp.

H. G. Wells, *Things to Come* (1935). With New Introductions by Allan Asherman and George Zebrowski, complete film credits and 16 stills from the film version. 184 pp.

G. McLeod Winsor, *Station X* (1919). With a New Introduction by Richard Gid Powers. 336 pp.

Eugene Zamiatin, *We* (1934). Translated from the Russian by Gregory Zilboorg, with Introductory Material by Peter Rudy, Marc Slonim, and Gregory Zilboorg, and a New Critical Afterword by Vasa D. Mihailovich. 272 pp.

Series II

Brian W. Aldiss, *Hothouse* (1962). With a New Introduction by Joseph Milicia. 272 pp.

Poul Anderson, *War of the Wing-Men* (1958). With New Introduction by Charles N. Brown and Sandra Miesel. 176 pp.

Anonymous, *Man Abroad* (1887). With a New Introduction by Lyman Tower Sargent. 88 pp.

D. G. Compton, *The Steel Crocodile* (1970). With a New Introduction by David G. Hartwell. 240 pp.

Joseph Conrad and Ford Madox Hueffer, *The Inheritors* (1901). With a New Introduction by Elaine L. Kleiner. 352 pp.

C. I. Defontenay, *Star* (1854). Translated from the French by P. J. Sokolowski, with New Introductions by Pierre Versins and Marc Angenot. 208 pp.

Samuel R. Delany, *Babel-17* (1966). With a New Introduction by Robert Scholes. 176 pp.

Samuel R. Delany, *The Jewels of Aptor* (1967). With a New Introduction by Don Hausdorff. 176 pp.

Philip K. Dick, *Solar Lottery* (1955). With a New Introduction by Thomas M. Disch. 208 pp.

Thomas M. Disch, *334* (1974). With a New Introduction by M. John Harrison. 288 pp.

Ellsworth Douglass, *Pharaoh's Broker* (1899). With a New Introduction by Richard A. Lupoff. 336 pp.

Jack Finney, *The Body Snatchers* (1955). With a New Introduction by Richard Gid Powers and 16 stills from the film, *Invasion of the Body Snatchers.* 224 pp.

Daniel F. Galouye, *Dark Universe* (1961). With a New Introduction by Robert Thurston. 176 pp.

David G. Hartwell and L. W. Currey editors, *The Battle of the Monsters and Other Stories: An Anthology of American Science Fiction.* With an Introduction and Notes on Stories by the editors. 240 pp.

Fritz Leiber, *The Big Time* (1961). With a New Introduction by Robert Thurston. 144 pp.

Michael Moorcock, *The Final Programme* (1968). With a New Introduction by Norman Spinrad. 184 pp.

R. D. Mullen and Darko Suvin, editors, *Science-Fiction Studies: Selected Articles on Science Fiction, 1973–1975.* With a Preface and Notes by the editors. 320 pp.

Alexei Panshin. *Rite of Passage* (1968). With a New Introduction by Alexei Panshin. 272 pp.

Joanna Russ, *Alyx* (1976). An original collection of all stories and the novel *Picnic on Paradise* featuring the character Alyx. With a New Introduction by Samuel R. Delany. 288 pp.

David Russen, *Iter Lunare* (1703). With a New Introduction by Mary Elizabeth Bowen. 168 pp.

Norman Spinrad, editor, *Modern Science Fiction: An Anthology* (1974). With a New Introduction by Thomas D. Clareson. 560 pp.

W. Olaf Stapledon, *Last Men in London* (1932). With a New Introduction by Curtis C. Smith and Harvey J. Satty. 336 pp.

Frank R. Stockton, *The Science Fiction of Frank R. Stockton: An Anthology*. Edited with a New Introduction by Richard Gid Powers. 352 pp.

Theodore Sturgeon, *Venus Plus X* (1960). With a New Introduction by Paul Williams. 176 pp.

James Tiptree, Jr., *10,000 Light-Years from Home* (1973). With a New Introduction by Gardner Dozois. 328 pp.

Jack Vance, *The Dragon Masters* (1962). With a New Introduction by Norman Spinrad. 128 pp.

Stanley Waterloo, *Armageddon* (1898). With a New Introduction by Richard Gid Powers. 280 pp.

Roger Zelazny, *The Dream Master* (1966). With a New Introduction by Ormond Seavey. 176 pp.

Roger Zelazny, *Isle of the Dead* (1969). With a New Introduction by Thomas F. Monteleone. 208 pp.

GREGG PRESS
A Division of G. K. Hall & Co.
70 Lincoln Street
Boston, Massachusetts 02111

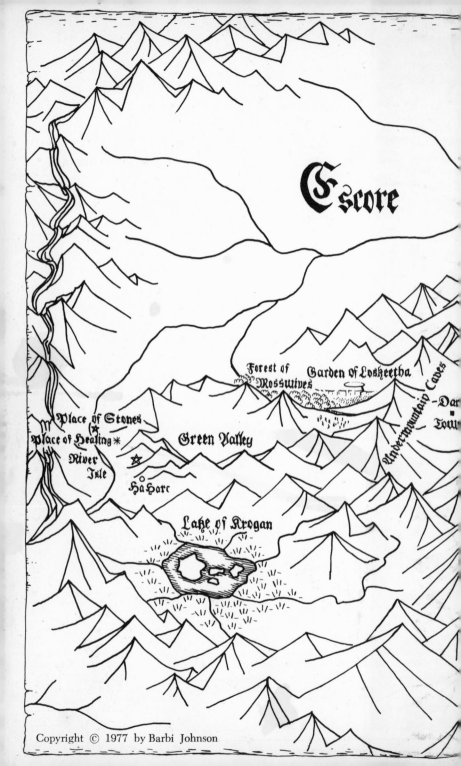

Escore

Forest of Mossmives

Garden of Loskeetha

Undermountain Caves

Dar · Tou·

Place of Stones
(☆)

Place of Healing ✳

River Isle

Green Valley

☆
Ha Hare

Lake of Krogan

Copyright © 1977 by Barbi Johnson